DEFENDERS OF HOPE

VOLUME 2

THE GREAT FORGET FANTASY SERIES

TERRY IRONWOOD

All rights reserved. No part of this publication may be reproduced, stored or transmitted in any form or by any means, electronic, mechanical, photocopying, recording, scanning, or otherwise without written permission from the publisher. It is illegal to copy this book, post it to a website, or distribute it by any other means without permission.

Copyright © 2024 by Terry Ironwood

This novel is entirely a work of fiction. The names, characters and incidents portrayed in it are the work of the author's imagination. Any resemblance to actual persons, living or dead, events or localities is entirely coincidental.

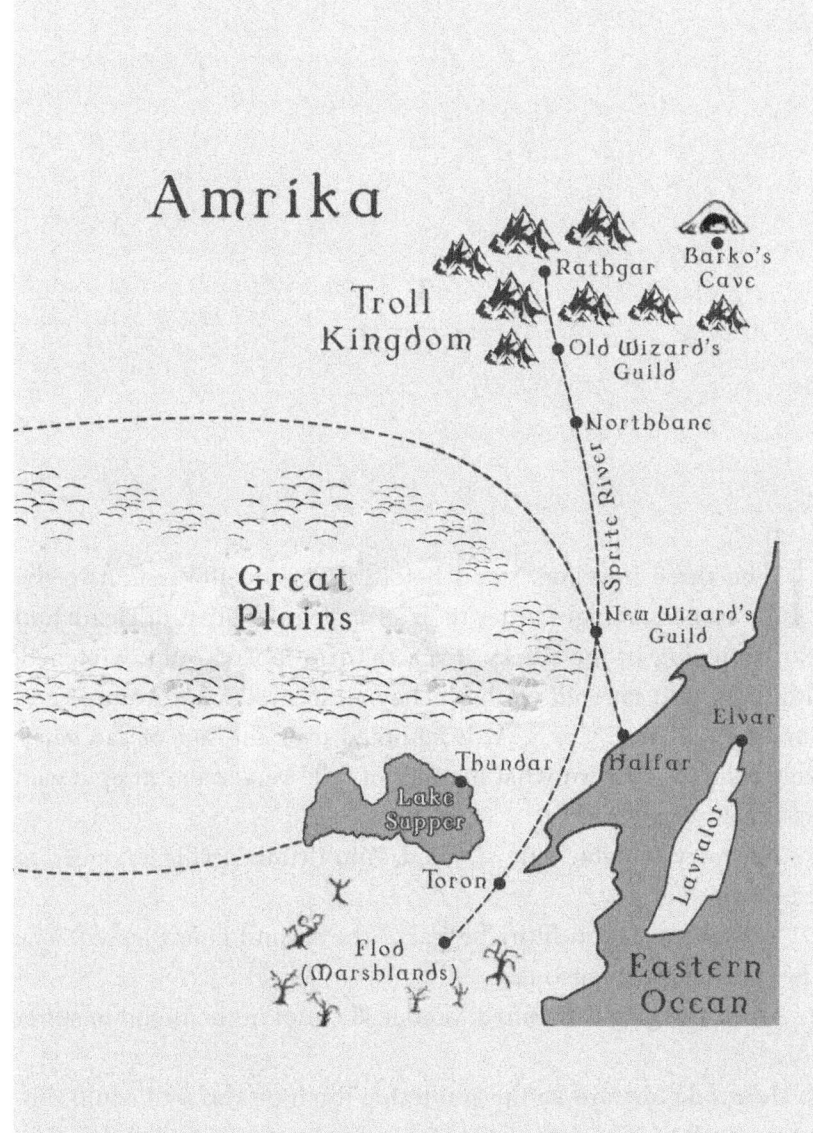

1

The three travellers stood before the gates of Vanalon in the darkness of night. After their struggle in the Pass of Death and near drowning in the Rocky River, the trio looked quite wretched, with filthy and tattered clothes. They all desired a warm meal and much-needed rest. The guards squinted over the top of the gates, likely trying to discern what manner of folk were attempting to gain passage at such a time.

"No entry tonight," one shouted. "You drunken villagers need to head home."

"Go sober up, you filthy beggars," the second guard jeered. The other one laughed raucously.

"Open the gates!" boomed Xander. "I'm not in the mood to suffer fools."

He strode forward so the sputtering torch on the wall could illuminate his face. The first guard recoiled with recognition and looked at his companion for support, but none was forthcoming. "I'm so sorry, Master Wizard. I did not recognize you. We have strict orders to keep the gates closed tonight, by order of King Rupert. Last night, someone lit the signal fire in the Pass of Death."

The second guard chimed in, "It was likely one of the watchmen tripping with a torch or igniting it with a lit pipe while drunk," he chortled, but his laughter died off as the man noticed the wizard's dark expression.

The first guard took a deep breath and gulped. It was apparent they were both inexperienced. "Even if it was an accident, we still cannot let you in by order of the king. He commanded that no one enter the gates but the scouting party he sent out early this morning to investigate the signal fire. No exceptions."

The weapons master walked forward out of the shadows. "Open the gates on orders of the High Commander of Vanalon." The first guard's jaw dropped. Garth casually rested his hand on his sword hilt. "I recognize you as a recent recruit from the front lines near the troll border. Your wealthy parents insisted you were not suited to fight the trolls and instead secured a safe position for you here in Vanalon." He paused. "I am afraid your parents chose wrong, as you will soon see. The boy behind me lit the signal fire. We come from the Pass of Death and must speak with our new king without delay. Now open the gates before our Grand Wizard here blasts you off the wall. He is not in a good mood."

The guards looked at each other, faces contorting. It was apparent they did not want to defy a direct order from King Rupert, but this was their commander standing with a wizard of legend. Furthermore, such a wizard would likely incinerate them if they did not comply. Nodding in unison, the soldiers decided wisely to open the gates.

"Our apologies, high commander," said the new recruit, coming down to meet him. "We will stay vigilant tonight and only open the gates upon the scouting party's return."

Garth strode past them without slowing. "They will not be returning."

The guard stood open-mouthed but said nothing. The weapons master stopped and turned. "Tell Captain Mack to stay up tonight no matter how late. I need to speak with him." The soldier nodded and saluted.

The small party continued down the main cobbled road towards the palace. On either side, shops displayed their wares, beckoning passersby with warm, bright light. Many were preparing to close for the evening.

Chip could smell the delicious aromas of spice cakes and chocolate wafers wafting from the abundant dessert shops. Those nostalgic odours were only overshadowed by the mouth-watering scent of lamb stew floating out of the taverns. The orphan realized how famished he was. They had lost their packs in the river and had not eaten since midday.

The people of Vanalon were friendly, and several waved in recognition at the high commander and Grand Wizard. Most stood agape at the condition of their clothes and hair. Some asked if they needed assistance, but Xander waved them off.

Chip watched the townsfolk bustling about to buy whatever last item they needed before retiring for the evening. The quaint frontier city attracted all manner of people from light-skinned to dark, fashionable to practical, and commoner to noble. Soldiers patrolled the streets at regular intervals, ensuring a safe environment for all. Many foreigners thronged to the city, especially in summer, but few stayed beyond the visitor season. Winters were cold, and the surrounding mountains were dangerous. Still, Vanalon's legendary hospitality attracted sightseers and adventurers from afar.

The boy's smile disappeared as he realized what was coming for the unsuspecting townsfolk. A darkness more sinister than anything they could imagine was about to envelop the small city. Everything was about to change.

They reached the main market square, which was almost deserted. During the day, there was a bustling throng of people, with hawkers selling their goods. Now, shuttered market stalls lined the perimeter. The centerpiece was a giant stone statue of a man holding aloft a mighty sword facing west to the Pass of Death. Most citizens, however, thought it was only symbolic.

They left the town center behind to enter a high-class district with stately three-storey apartments. These overlooked gleaming patterned stone walkways with perfectly spaced trees. Throughout the small city, beautiful fountains showcased each square.

The ground rose towards the palace, which appeared in the distance, perched on a low hill. As they neared their destination, the houses ended, and green gardens appeared.

The city was designed with a purpose in mind. Beautiful parkland surrounded the palace, which was visually pleasing yet also provided a clear view of any enemy. The walls of the castle were the secondary defence if the main walls were ever breached. The truth was that if the barrier fell, the defences of the small kingdom were woefully inadequate to withstand an assault by a demon army.

The real purpose of the city was to stall the enemy as long as possible while the rest of Amrika prepared. Despite that, few believed there was anything behind the barrier, especially after three thousand years. The people were content to live their happy, idyllic lives without a worry in the world. *Well, that was about to change*, Chip thought.

Past the gardens, the familiar white palace walls reflected the light of the torches spaced in sconces atop them. They approached the gorgeous wrought iron gate in the center. The weapons master saluted the guards, and they gained entry without question. One soldier ran on ahead to inform the king of their arrival. To the side was the empty training yard.

Chip had sparred here countless evenings over the years. A ring of torches surrounded the area, illuminating the stables where the boy lived. If they had horses, they would have left them here. Chip felt a pang of sadness for the animals who had fallen in the demon attack on the bridge.

The small party mounted the steps to the palace entrance, which opened into a quaint foyer. A long hallway led to two beautiful, gilded doors with a guard on either side. The squire greeted them as they entered. It was Chase's father, Mr. Longfellow, who winked at Chip, his son's best friend, and led them down the hall. He nodded to the guards, knocked once, and then ceremoniously pushed open both doors to reveal a large throne room.

Two giant hearths with low simmering fires warmed the polished stone floor. A long oak table sat in the middle of the room. Instead of sitting at the head of this table, King Rupert lounged on the intricately carved wooden throne at the far end, one of his legs casually draped over the arm of the great chair. Queen Charlotte sat to his right, looking embarrassed. Chip's eyes widened to see Princess Eleanor on his left.

For a moment, her beauty took him aback. They had been friends since he began school, but now, he could see her changing before his eyes. He covered his surprise and nodded to her with a slight grin. She looked apprehensive, which was unusual. On both sides stood six guards, which seemed unnecessary. Worse, three of them were Rupert's friends from school: Biff, Chubs, and Gunter. The king must have promoted them to his private guard despite never training a day in their lives.

Xander assessed the situation and strode forward to stand before the new king, making the slightest of bows. The high commander and the boy followed suit. Rupert gloated as he watched Chip bow before him.

"Hail, King Rupert. I know you are still grieving the loss of your father, but we come with urgent news," Xander said.

The new king lazily removed his leg from the arm of the throne and leaned forward. "The news can wait. Did Chip complete his quest?" He failed to hide his smug smile.

"He did, but grave circumstances have arisen that need immediate attention," the wizard intoned.

"Great," Rupert replied with an arrogant grin. "Then I can assign him to a profession." The other three guards snickered loudly but quieted at the wizard's glare.

"The Autumn Harvest Ceremony is not for another month. This is not the time..." the wizard began, but the king held up his hand.

"I assign Chip to the profession of kitchen help for the remainder of his life, under the care and guidance of Miss Stern." He beamed. "To begin immediately." The guards could not control their laughter, and King Rupert's ponderous belly jiggled in mirth. He motioned for the guards to escort the boy to the kitchens.

Chip seethed with anger and almost shattered the Wall in his mind, then remembered the wizard's stern warning not to reveal his magic. As the guards moved forward to approach him with smug faces, Xander raised his hand, palm outward. The look on his face could have stopped a fanged black bear.

"This is not going to happen. Get back to your posts," Xander spoke calmly, but the power in his voice was unmistakable." The king opened his mouth in shock, but before he could speak, the wizard continued in a louder voice, directing his gaze at Rupert. "Your entire watch at the Pass of Death is dead. The barrier has been breached and is failing fast. Chip found the six watchmen torn to pieces by a demon horde. He managed to light the signal fire before they turned on him. The boy fought bravely and slew many. The high commander and I arrived while he was battling them single-handed. We killed the entire horde, including their Dark Elf leader. Word of this will spread through the ranks like quick-fire. Do you want to be known as the king whose first command is to send the hero of the kingdom to the kitchens to satisfy a childhood rivalry?"

King Rupert shrank as the wizard's voice grew in volume. The guards stepped backwards. Queen Charlotte hid a small smile. Princess Eleanor nodded in satisfaction.

"Well, I mean..." stammered the king. Xander stepped closer. The guards did not dare intercede.

"The Wizard's Guild appointed me to Vanalon with the blessing of High King Dominor of Toron, your grand uncle. I was there when he was born. The legacy of all your ancestors falls upon your shoulders, Rupert. A demon assassin killed your father two nights ago. You have the chance to avenge his death. The very fate of humankind hinges on your actions. We have all pledged to defend Vanalon and the land of Amrika if the barrier is ever breached. Well, that time is now!" The wizard stepped back to let his words sink in.

The entire room fell silent. King Rupert's shock at hearing that a demon assassinated his father seemed to sober him up. A look of anger, then fear, battled for control across his chubby face. He looked like nothing more than a spoiled brat whose sense of entitlement and selfish worldview was crumbling before the grim reality of life.

The king looked around at his mother and sister for help, but they wisely let him work through the enormity of the wizard's words. Struggling, Rupert tried one last time to discount the story and hang on to his disintegrating reality.

"How do you know for sure the barrier is failing?" he asked timidly.

Xander eyed the king's obvious discomfort, and a look of sadness crossed his face. He leaned forward and spoke softly, "Because I helped build it."

Rupert looked surprised, then finally nodded as if in a stupor.

"What would you have me do, Grand Wizard?" he asked.

Xander scrutinized him for a moment without answering then nodded in satisfaction. "First and foremost, send a message to King Henry of Calgar to send reinforcements immediately. We cannot hope to defeat the demon hordes here in Vanalon, but we can delay their advance to allow the other cities time to prepare. Ask for one thousand men. When we abandon the city, we can retreat in a fashion that slows their advance. Warn the surrounding villagers of the impending attack and have them leave for Calgar immediately. It is a one-week walk. Ask King Henry to provide refuge for those who seek it.

"Next, draft a message to High King Dominor in the capital to send reinforcements to Calgar, at least five thousand. That will be the second line of defence when Vanalon is overrun. A strong stand made in Calgar will also slow the demon hordes before it, too, is abandoned. From there, the remaining army will retreat to Toron, where we will fight the Last Battle.

"The lands around the walls of Vanalon are woefully inadequate for defence. We must dig trenches, set traps, and provide our archers with easy targets. Anything that slows the demons' momentum helps to achieve this. Third, send word to my brother Balor at the Guild. Tell him to send wizards for assistance. They can wait at Calgar, as they cannot make it to Vanalon in time. Magic wielders will be instrumental in limiting our damages.

"The Demon King has a powerful Inner Circle of eleven Dark

Elves and a fearsome general named Morgo. In the initial assault, I suspect he will include one or two of the Inner Circle to command the first demon horde. We have already met Elohan, who is a member. If the Unnamed One sends General Morgo, then the Creator help us. For now, the barrier is very weak but still holds. Even so, hundreds can slip through. It will take at least one week for the reinforcements to arrive from Calgar. We must pray the demons do not attack before then."

The king listened gravely and then nodded. He looked sad and lost. "I'm going to lose my kingdom, aren't I?" he asked, already knowing the answer.

Xander nodded grimly. "I'm afraid so. Nonetheless, never lose hope. Vanalon can one day be restored. Your actions in the next few weeks will make or break you, King Rupert. I know you are young, but this is your chance to be a true king who makes a difference to the very fate of humankind. Queen Charlotte and your sister are prudent and much wiser than you think. Heed their advice."

"We will assist in any way we can," the queen offered. Princess Eleanor nodded and smiled in agreement. Chip felt his heart brighten as their eyes met.

The weapons master stepped forward. "My king," he intoned formally. "I ask leave to make preparations with Captain Mack."

The king gestured his approval. "You have leave, high commander."

Garth looked to the wizard, who nodded, then turned and left the throne room.

Xander cleared his throat. "Chip has had a harrowing journey. I ask for the use of a guest suite where we can eat and rest tonight. I would talk with him regarding information he has collected from the Inner Circle member Elohan, among other things. I want you to know that your father's death has been avenged. At base camp, Chip killed the three-toed demon that assassinated him." The king digested this new information. Several emotions played across his face.

Finally, Rupert sighed. "Thank you, Chip, for your service to the kingdom. We need all swords for this battle. Yours is welcome. I rescind your duties in the kitchen and designate you as a soldier of Vanalon, Chase too. We will talk more tomorrow."

Chip's eyes widened. Rupert's friends showed surprise, yet even they grudgingly looked at him with newfound respect. The orphan and the wizard bowed again, taking their leave. Xander's bow was much deeper this time, indicating his approval of the king's change of heart.

Squire Longfellow escorted the pair to the guest rooms. The man was tall with a perfect posture. He winked at Chip, who grinned. He had met Chase's dad often in the training yard when he dropped by to observe their drills. He was kind and always provided encouragement.

"Chase wants to hear everything as soon as possible," the squire whispered in Chip's ear when they left the throne room. "Since you left on your quest, my son has shown agitation. When the signal fire was lit, he volunteered to assist the scouting party sent this morning to investigate, but Captain Mack refused. He's been in a sulk ever since." They turned right down a long, polished stone corridor leading to the palace's north wing.

"Tell Chase I will talk to him tomorrow, Mr. Longfellow. Let him know that the scouting party is dead. He is lucky Captain Mack kept him here. I will explain when I see him." The boy's response startled the squire. He was about to ask more, but after a glance at the wizard, simply nodded. They turned left at the end of the corridor and arrived at a series of panelled wood doors. The squire led them to the first one on the left. There was a gold lock on the door. He produced a key from a pocket in his tunic and smoothly inserted it in the lock.

There was an audible click as the squire turned the handle and opened the door to a beautifully furnished room boasting a large hearth and lavish chairs. Two doors at the back opened to the sleeping quarters. "I will ready the baths," Mr. Longfellow said, disappearing into the bedrooms. The oak-panelled room featured intricately carved furniture. Chip caught his breath at the exquisite paintings adorning the walls and the rich, plush carpeting. He had never stayed in a room so beautiful. The boy realized with a start that he had never stayed in an actual room before or slept in a real bed, for that matter. The wizard glanced at him and laughed.

"If you think this is nice, wait until you see the Grand Palace in Toron, or the Guild, for that matter." When the squire returned, the wizard gestured for him to light the fire. "Mr. Longfellow, could you be so kind as to bring us two heaping plates from the kitchen? We are famished. Also, two glasses of mulled wine."

Chase's father bowed. "At once, Mr. Wizard." He left and closed the door without a sound. The fire had caught and was already shedding light and warmth to the room. Xander sat wearily in one of the two plush chairs by the hearth. Chip tentatively sat in the other, marvelling at the feel of the soft leather. The boy had lived his whole life in a pantry or stable room. Here, he felt like the wealthiest noble.

"You did well, Chip," the wizard began. "Up at base camp, I told you I would try to answer your questions. There are important things you do not know, even about yourself. But first, did you see anything important in Elohan's memories on the bridge? You were silent for several moments when his presence entered your mind, and then I saw a look of fear on his face. I did not interfere until I observed the Dark Elf recoil. I wanted to give you time to glean information. That is when I unleashed my magic. I was strong enough to injure him, but Elohan surprised me with the speed at which he recovered and summoned the lightning bolt. His strength has grown. Were you able to learn anything from him?"

The wizard leaned forward with his piercing blue eyes.

The boy recalled the harrowing confrontation on the bridge. "I felt his presence enter my mind, trying to see my Power, so I wrapped him in the Calm," Chip said. The wizard's eyes widened. "He seemed unaware I was there, so I delved into his memories. Time seemed to slow. I saw him as a young elf being swayed by an evil older elf prince named Kill..."

"Don't!" commanded the wizard. "Do not utter that name. He is the Unnamed One, the King of the Dark Elves and the King of the Demons. Pick your title, but do not say his true name. You are but a handful of people who even know his birth name. His Power is so great the mere mention of it directs his gaze. There would be no risk if the barrier were whole, but now..." Xander held up his hands. "Carry on."

Chip nodded and let his heart settle after Xander's sudden admonishment.

The boy continued, "The Unnamed One showed Elohan and other elves how to secretly remove the Walls to their Power permanently. As time passed, their eyes turned black. The group was discovered, and the Elf Council met to discuss punishment. They banished the Unnamed One and his followers, but the elf prince killed his father, King Galal, instead of leaving. The young prince tried to take control, but they were outnumbered and driven out, settling west in the caves high in the mountains northwest of Calgar. They began reproducing, but their offspring were deformed and became known as the demon race. The weak were fed to the stronger ones."

Chip shuddered and went on, "Occasionally, a white-eyed demon was born with the Power. Elohan watched the Demon King harvest these demon babies and drink their Power in a sinister ritual where he… ate them. Sometimes, he shared. Now that I think of it, someone else was also there. He wore a black cloak and stood in the background. I could not see his face, but they called him Morgo." Xander jolted upright. A look of dismay crossed his features.

"It is as I feared," the wizard said. "The Unnamed One has found a way to increase his Power. No demon has the use of magic, but some rare ones with white eyes are still born with it, even though they are unable to access it. He has found a way to harvest their Power through the Dark Arts. The black-cloaked figure you saw in the memory is General Morgo, who studied fell practices over the millennia. We do not know what he is, but we know he is a creature to fear. I suspect now that the barrier was never weakening on its own. Instead, the Unnamed One has grown too strong to be contained." He let the enormity of the statement hang.

"Then how do we stop him?" Chip finally asked.

"Not me, you," he answered. The boy gave him a puzzled look. Suddenly, they heard a loud knock at the door. Chip nearly jumped out of his skin.

"Come in," said Xander. He had an amused look on his face at the boy's reaction. Mr. Longfellow entered carrying a large tray that he placed on the table between them. In the middle was a delicious-smelling steaming pot of lamb stew next to a loaf of fresh bread and a small bowl of butter. Two full glasses of mulled wine accompanied the dish. The squire ladled two heaping servings in each bowl and placed the wine in front.

"Enjoy, gentlemen," he bowed and briefly revisited the bedrooms to tend to the baths then reappeared and excused himself. The wizard put down his glass and cut the bread then handed a piece to Chip. Without saying a word, the boy smeared a healthy dose of butter on one side and took a large bite. It must have just come out of the oven. He dug into the hot stew, savouring its richness. The orphan could not remember being so hungry. He washed it down with the mulled wine and almost spit it out. Eleanor had snuck ale with Chase and him a few times but never wine. It was something meant for older gentlemen or nobles.

He forced himself to continue sipping it and surprisingly began to change his mind on the taste. Perhaps he could get used to it after all. The boy looked up to see the wizard inhaling his meal. After they had both helped themselves to a second bowl, Chip pushed back his chair and allowed himself a respite.

"What did you mean by me, not you?" he asked casually, hoping he had misheard.

"Exactly what I said," responded the wizard. Chip waited. The old man continued to eat.

Finally, trying not to sound exasperated, Chip asked, "Could you elaborate?" Xander looked up innocently. He took another bite then pushed back his bowl and reached for his pipe. The boy groaned inwardly. He knew that cataclysmic statements were about to be uttered whenever the wizard lit his pipe.

The orphan took a deep breath and watched the wizard light it with his finger then draw in a satisfying pull of tobacco. Xander let it out in a scented cloud that dissipated throughout the room. The fire was going strong, and the flames danced shadows across his lined face.

"The Demon King was born with red eyes," he stated. Chip nodded once, trying to subdue a mounting fear. The only sound was of the fire crackling in the hearth. Xander took another pull of his pipe. "He was the only elf to be born in such a way. The elven wise ones searched for meaning in all their texts but found none. They asked the world of men to look in their libraries to find a clue. No one could discover why an elven prince was born with red eyes in all the books, scrolls, and letters. They even looked back to the Great Forget." The wizard took a sip of wine, peering over the rim.

"The Great Forget?" the boy asked.

"It is the moment in time when our memories begin."

Chip nodded, remembering his history lessons. "In school, Miss Owl called it The Beginning, meaning the start of recorded history. She said it is all speculation about what happened before then. One theory was that the races were all illiterate five millennia ago, and parchment had not been created."

The wizard studied him. "She has been told to say that." The boy looked puzzled.

"Why? And by whom?"

"That is not important right now. Just understand that it is a term wizards use to describe a wall in time if you will. All our books throughout the lands go back to a certain time, and then there is nothing before it. There are no records, no stories, no oral traditions passed down for generations, nothing. It is as if we never existed."

The wizard leaned forward. "All we know is that a great magical event occurred that wiped out everyone's memory."

Chip's eyes widened. "How is that possible?"

"We do not know," Xander answered. "The Guild was close to finding out millennia ago, but then the Great Battle occurred, and we lost our most powerful members. The furthest they had discerned was that some unknown Power had created the Great Forget. The council did identify an ancient underground city that might have the answers. Unfortunately, not even the wizards of old were strong enough to enter, including our most powerful members. An unknown creature of terrifying power guarded the entrance.

"News of this reached the Unnamed One, so he captured and tortured one of our council members, thereby extracting the location of the entrance. Being the most powerful wielder of magic in the world, he wanted the riches and knowledge of this city. No one guards something of little worth, so the Demon King knew if he could make it past this creature or guardian, he would have great rewards."

The wizard paused and pulled on his pipe. This gave Chip a chance to jump in. He desperately wanted to ask about his red eyes, but the boy also wanted to hear the end of the story. He was about to ask anyway, but Xander raised his hand.

"Patience, my boy. Your questions may be answered in the telling." Chip nodded and signalled for the wizard to continue, trying to be patient. The old man resumed, "There are underground tunnels below the vast capital city of Toron. Beneath the tunnels is a much older city with tunnels of its own. That story is for another time. The important point is that deep below that second city is a truly ancient city. Its name is unknown. Few even know it exists. For now, we call it the Ancient City. It took many years to find the entrance, and even then, it took luck and persistence. The city was discovered by a very powerful old wizard named Arkan over three millennia ago on the advice of a group of Seers."

Chip looked perplexed.

"Seers can sense magic and have the power of Telling the future," the wizard explained, seeing the boy's look. "Charlatans abound, so it is hard for most to tell a true Seer. However, all true Seers can sense the Power. So a magic user can at least verify if the Seer can sense, which is the first requirement for authenticity." Chip thought he understood and nodded.

Xander carried on, "Several true Seers gave Arkan clues to the entrance of the fabled city. Even so, he only received fragments of the Telling from each Seer. It was as if the powers that be were unwilling to bestow all the answers at once. Only after many years was he able to piece together enough fragments to decipher where the entrance was hidden. He felt the Ancient City would hold the answers to the Great Forget. He finally located the entrance and tried to open it, but a strange creature with immense power blocked him from entering.

"Arkan fought valiantly but could not defeat this guardian and retreated, barely escaping with his life. When he reported his findings to the council, the city's existence was leaked to the Unnamed One from an unknown source. The Demon King captured a wizard from the council and tortured the location out of him. He then went to Toron to find the underground entrance to the Ancient City. Find it he did."

Incredibly, the wizard ladled himself another bowl of stew. Chip tried to control his patience as the old man also helped himself to another slice of bread. The boy even watched him butter it before he blurted.

"And then what happened!"

The wizard looked up in surprise. He placed the buttered bread by his bowl and leaned back. "My goodness, just trying to eat a little food. Where were we? Oh, the Demon King was confronted by the creature guarding the Ancient City. Long he battled it, and deep were his wounds, but eventually, he triumphed. The Dark Elf King was so weak after the struggle that he had to crawl through the entrance. He barely had the strength to use his magic to light the way. The Unnamed One wandered ancient streets and found a building with artifacts of incredible Power. It was a huge structure made of blocks of light brown stone with a tower in the middle. One talisman healed him of his weariness and restored his magic.

"Despite this, even at full strength, he was still not strong enough to wield some of the other artifacts and could not remove any of them from the building. He wondered who could have made such a city. The Demon King found a library next to the building and entered. It was three stories tall with a grand entrance. He found a book called

The Great Forget, though something stopped him from reading it. He would not discuss what it was even with his Inner Circle.

"He continued to the center of the city where two curved buildings many stories high surrounded a circular structure. He entered to find a vast white round room. At the far end was a high-backed chair, similar to a throne. In it sat the unmoving body of what appeared to be a great dead king wearing resplendent armour the likes of which he had never seen. The gauntleted hand held a sword with a red stone on the hilt.

"There was a huge white table in front of the ancient king with one object resting on it, a red box. The Unnamed One opened the box and, nestled on a crimson cushion inside, was an... orb pulsating with light. He could not resist lifting the orb, so he reached in and seized it. As he did, the Demon King sensed something awaken of enormous Power. He looked up to see the dead king's eyes had opened and shone red through the visor of his helmeted head. It spoke to him in a voice of raw Power. 'Even if you escape me, one other will be born with red eyes who will shake the Earth. Only one red-eye will survive. Now die.' The king then stood, well over eight feet tall."

The wizard helped himself to a heaping spoon of stew, chewing happily. Chip clenched his hands in frustration. Seeing the boy's reaction, the wizard scowled and set the bowl down.

"The Unnamed One fled. He heard the Red-Eyed King emit a terrifying howl of rage, the sound of which burst both his eardrums. He instinctively reached into the orb and used its Power to flee. It gave him unmatched speed and strengthened his own Power. He now had a weapon that gave him the advantage he needed to defeat the wizards and the Light Elves combined." He paused to take another bite of stew. Chip mulled this over, unsure of something.

"How do we know all this?" the boy finally asked.

"Simple. The wizards high above in Toron sensed the Demon King's battle with the guardian. They knew someone had attempted to breach the Ancient City. After the Unnamed One escaped back to his people in the caves, we abducted a member of his Inner Circle.

Look at it as retribution for the torturing of our own council member. This Dark Elf was persuaded to tell the full story, which the Demon King had revealed to him. We also learned the timing of the impending attack on Amrika, which led to the Great Battle on the plains. Before the battle, we devised a plan."

Xander shovelled in the remaining few bites in his bowl and smiled in satisfaction. Chip rolled his eyes.

"So, what was the plan?"

The wizard picked up his wine glass and leaned back. "Glad you asked. A young wizard was sent to steal the orb from the Demon King on the eve of the battle on the Great Plains. With the aid of the council's magic, he was made to appear as the Dark Inner Circle Elf Elohan." The boy's eyes widened. "The guise was almost perfect. The Elohan imposter distracted another part of the camp and drew the Unnamed One out of his royal tent to investigate the commotion. The imposter then walked calmly towards the two demons left guarding the entrance.

"They recognized him as Elohan and allowed entry, but both looked very confused. Almost immediately, one of them followed him in. As the fake Elohan entered, he turned around and sent a small line of blue magic through the demon's eye, melting his brain. The young wizard imposter then realized someone else was in the tent with him and came face to face with the real Elohan, who stood open-mouthed. As the story goes, the imposter asked himself, 'What are the odds of running into Elohan when I am impersonating him?' The second demon rushed in and looked at both Elohans in utter confusion. It even peed itself, such was the creature's consternation."

Xander slapped his thigh and let out a boisterous laugh then reached for another piece of bread. Chip stared at him in exasperation.

"Well, what did the imposter do?" the boy asked. "And how do you know all this?" Something about Xander's interaction with Elohan on the bridge jogged his memory. He eyed the wizard suspiciously. "How did Elohan know your name on the bridge? Why did he say he missed you?" Xander said nothing as he chewed his bread, but his eyes sparkled with mirth. "How do you know what the young wizard was thinking, Xandrostika?"

"Clever lad," the old man murmured, leaning forward. "I was the young wizard."

"How is that possible?" Chip exclaimed. "You would be three thousand years old!"

"Give or take," Xander agreed.

"But ..."

The old wizard sighed. "I am old, my boy. Almost older than any human left, save my brother. You see, magic wielders do not live normal lives. We age very slowly. Those with greater Power age even slower. The Unnamed One was already centuries old when I stole the orb. He looked almost the same as when the Light Elves banished him. It is possible that even now, he has not aged much."

Chip shook his head in wonder, then a realization hit him like a lightning bolt.

"What about me?" he asked.

The wizard studied him. "You, dear boy, may be the longest-living human ever." Chip reeled. Mixed emotions flooded his mind. "Do not dwell on it for now. A war is coming, the likes of which the world has never seen. If nothing befalls you, then you can worry about your mortality."

The boy forced himself to put the unnerving ramifications aside.

"So what did the real Elohan do when you stood before him?" Chip asked, his curiosity getting the better of him.

"Oh, I threw a ball of fire at him and the remaining demon. Elohan was able to dive out of the way and erect a shield in time, but the force slammed him into a heavy table, knocking him out. I thought he was dead. The demon, having no defence to my magic, died a fiery death. I then found the Orb of Power in a black box on a table in the corner and slit the back wall of the royal tent, slipping out unnoticed. My guise remained intact, and no one questioned me as I exited the camp. I did hear a huge commotion as I reached the perimeter, which told me the Demon King had returned to find the orb missing."

He leaned back with a smile of satisfaction.

"Why do I have red eyes when I use magic?" Chip asked, face frozen in anticipation. "I want to know." The wizard looked at him in surprise, then compassion.

"I wish I had all the answers, my boy," Xander said. Chip's shoulders slumped. "But I can tell you what I do know. There are only three instances of a red-eyed magic wielder since the Great Forget—the Unnamed One, the Red-Eyed King, and now you. When someone abandoned you as a baby at the gates of Vanalon sixteen summers ago, Queen Charlotte sent a message to me at the Wizard's Guild. She used a messenger pigeon, saying a baby with red eyes had been discovered. I decided to come here with my Protector a few months later to verify.

"You had bright red eyes for the first six months of your life. It was disturbing for some, and they tried to remove you due to their superstitious beliefs. I asked Queen Charlotte to put you with someone she trusted. She wisely chose the master midwife Auntie Clare. You needed to experience a loving caregiver in your early years. When your eyes switched to green at six months, I decided to stay here at Vanalon to continue monitoring you, as I frankly needed a break from the Wizard's Guild. Garth agreed to train you when you came of age. At eight years old, they put you in the kitchens to work. The king was adamant, and it was not a proper time to intercede, so I allowed it. It also taught you about the harsh realities of life."

"You allowed me to be a captive under that witch for two years?" Chip asked incredulously. "You could have stopped it." The boy's eyes became wet and filled with rage. The wizard's eyes widened, and then his voice took on an edge.

"Listen carefully, Chip," he said. "Life is not about happiness and comfort. You experienced all the negative aspects of life in those two years for a reason. I had to allow you to know what that feels like. Without it, you would never appreciate what we have and what we must fight for. I waited for you to break under the oppression of Miss Stern so I could intervene. To be honest, I could not believe it took you two years to show your rage. It is a testament to your strength, but it almost killed you. Only on your last legs did you seek retaliation. It was then that I intervened before the king when he pronounced judgment. I took you away from that miserable life and gave you to the weapons master to begin training.

"In the beginning, he trained you mercilessly, testing your limits. Even he took three full weeks to break you, and you were still a child. It was imperative to teach you, of all people, not to give up. Do you realize you never would have wanted to complete your training if you did not have all that misery to spur you on? You know from your lessons that only through discomfort do we grow, learn, and understand gratitude."

Chip's rage lessened as the wizard spoke, then vanished as a grudging understanding swept over him. Xander leaned forward. "Very few men, let alone boys, could have withstood the rigours of Garth's training. Almost all would have quit or failed. To you, the training was a much better life than you had previously known. I am sorry you had to go through all that, but it was necessary. I must admit it was too close a call for my liking, but your experience with Death may have been destined." Chip nodded as a realization swept through him.

"So you came to Vanalon because of me?" he asked with a look of wonder. He had never thought himself special. "I hope I have not disappointed you."

"Disappointed?" The wizard let out a deep laugh. "My goodness, my boy. You have shown more restraint than anybody I have ever known. You have trained without complaint for six years, showing tremendous growth and dedication. You displayed unparalleled bravery lighting the signal fire, knowing it was likely your last act. You singlehandedly fought a horde of demons, killing their Dark Elf captain. Disappointed? No. I could not be more proud." He smiled warmly, raising his glass in salute, and took a long drink of mulled wine. Chip raised his, too, letting the praise sink in. The world suddenly looked a whole lot different, and he felt a confidence he had never known.

"So, how can my red eyes make such a difference?"

"Well, we know that red is after blue for magic wielders. We surmised this when the Unnamed One was more powerful than anyone we had ever known. By all accounts, the Red-Eyed King in the Ancient City may be the most powerful being alive, as even the Unnamed One had to flee. Since we do not know if the underground king is human, or even a king for that matter, the title of the only human Red Level magic wielder falls to you. When you stopped Death from pulling your spirit essence into the netherworld, I saw your eyes blaze red in your mind. I needed to know what this could mean and immediately searched for the answer. Since all known libraries had been scoured for knowledge of red eyes, I went to the only place that may have the answer." Chip leaned forward.

"You went to the Ancient City!" he blurted. The wizard scowled.

"You just ruined my story. You are too clever." Xander rolled his eyes. "I assumed that since the Unnamed One had defeated the guardian of the Ancient City three thousand years ago when he stole the orb, it was reasonable to believe the Red-Eyed King was dead, so it would be safe to enter, right?"

He grimaced and hid behind his glass. It was Chip's turn to roll his eyes.

"I guess you were wrong," the boy stated, trying not to laugh.

"My goodness, right again." Xander coughed uncomfortably. "At least the guardian at the entrance was gone, so it was easy to get in. Plus, I used all the magic I could muster to disguise myself as a rat."

"A rat?" Chip asked.

"Yes, a rat." The wizard seemed embarrassed. "Well, not physically. I'm not a shapeshifter. I meant figuratively." Chip looked even more confused. "In case a mind probed for life forms in the vicinity, I used my magic to conceal myself as a rat, or the appearance of a rat. It did work for a while. I felt a powerful presence continuously scouring the city. It passed over me twice. I managed to find what had once been a magnificent library. Once inside, I could even make out a faint disturbance in the dirt and dust, which was likely made by the Unnamed One when he had entered three thousand years before. I found a book on the floor by the entrance. It must have rested on a great podium that stood directly before the door. Behind it was a room so vast I could not see the back wall. In it were hundreds of thousands of books. I picked up the one on the floor and found it contained lines of prophecy on the first page. The title was *The Great Forget*."

The boy's eyes widened as he leaned forward, not wishing to miss a single word.

With a far-off look, the wizard continued, "At that exact moment, as I gripped the book, about to read the most important truths of humankind, the presence passed over me again. This time, it paused. I decided to leave with the book and read it when I was safely away, but as I passed the entrance, the book fell to the floor of its own accord. I could not take it with me. I realized that the same thing must have happened to the Demon King. That is why it was lying there in the first place. I then tried to go into the room and grab another book, but an invisible wall of force prevented me from entering. A barrier had been erected behind the podium, which I could not pass. I decided to try and read the first few lines of the book on the floor before I was found out. However, it was too late.

"The presence blasted away my cover, and I heard a distant scream of rage. I managed to read the lines on the first page and then sensed something incredibly powerful coming closer. I ran full tilt out the library door and down to the end of the street. I turned around to find the Red-Eyed King bearing down on me with a mighty sword. He screamed something at me, and the force of his voice pushed me through the entrance. I landed quite literally on my bottom in the tunnel beyond." The wizard rubbed his backside with a scowl.

Chip waited, but the old man seemed lost in thought.

"So, what did he scream at you?" the boy finally asked in exasperation.

"Oh, he said, and I quote, 'Bring Him to me.'"

"Who's Him?"

"Not too bright now, are we?"

"Me?"

"Yes, you."

"Why?" the boy asked, perplexed.

The wizard gave him an insufferable look. "I assume it has something to do with your red eyes," he panned.

Chip considered this and nodded. "Makes sense, I suppose. Alright, so what did the first few lines of *The Great Forget* book say?" The question made Xander's amused look turn deadly serious.

The wizard cleared his throat.

"Herein lies the knowledge of the Great Forget,

Only the Red-Eyed One can make them remember,

Only He can read the words,

If He chooses,

And only when one Red-Eye is left,

All others who turn the page will die."

2

Chip waited for more. Then, seeing none forthcoming, he sat back and pondered the words.

"Well," Xander finally said, draining the rest of his mulled wine, "that settles it. I am tired." He waited for a response, then scowled at the boy. "My goodness, I was hoping for some insight," he grumbled. When Chip looked at him blankly, the wizard elaborated, "To the lines in the book."

"Oh, that," the boy yawned. "I guess it means I'm losing an eye or something, or two of us need to die to leave one left. Can I go to bed?"

The wizard glared at him, and then his look softened. "Very well. You deserve it. Rest now. Tomorrow, we start preparing."

A quiet knock sounded at the door. The wizard pushed himself up and opened it a crack, peering through, then smiled and pulled it fully open. Queen Charlotte slipped in and motioned for Xander to close the door behind her. He complied as he bowed and offered her his seat. Chip rose awkwardly and bowed the best he could.

"Now, now. No need for that." She waved for both to sit. "May I speak freely?" she asked, looking at the wizard with a penetrating gaze.

A look passed between them. "The boy is the one," Xander said without preamble. "He knows much already. We can trust him." The queen let out a long sigh and nodded with a satisfied smile.

She turned to Chip. "Despite what you think, I have watched over you for a long time. When you arrived as a babe, I immediately sent a message to Xander at the Wizard's Guild informing him of your red eyes. In the days of High Wizard Arkan, a wise Seer prophesized the coming of one with red eyes to provide balance. The Guild has been looking for you ever since. There were some isolated reports over the millennia of babies with red eyes, but they turned out to be false. Xander respected my intuition and came in person with the weapons master to investigate you. He decided to settle here and let the Guild know he would keep an eye on you and the Pass of Death at the same time. He also needed a much overdue break from the Guild and his overbearing brother, with whom he was often at odds."

She looked at Xander before continuing, "We watched you grow and saw your eyes change to green after six months. We surmised that your magic, if you truly had any, might go dormant until manhood. When you were ten summers, the magic seemed to surface early with Miss Stern and your experience with Death but then went dormant again. Interestingly, you have kept the ability to sense and feel magic the whole way through. You are special, Chip. I protected you from King Barton as much as I could. He was a selfish man but usually could be reasoned with, and deep down, there was some good in him. My son Rupert is similar and has no love for you. He did put his personal views aside tonight for the greater good when Xander confronted him, which shows promise. He still has much to learn. Your friend, Princess Eleanor, always defends you, as do I. We have high expectations of you."

The queen then walked up to him and lifted his chin. She turned his head this way and that. Chip felt self-conscious and realized how he must look. After two full days of fighting, running, and almost drowning, his clothes were in filthy tatters. Cuts and bruises covered his entire body, and dark circles ringed his eyes.

Queen Charlotte cupped his cheeks with both hands, and astonishingly, her eyes blazed yellow. Chip's eyes widened in wonder at the realization that the queen was a magic wielder. The boy felt a warm tingling spread over his entire body. He lifted his hands and watched his cuts close and fade away. His deeper wounds from the battle on the pass tingled and disappeared. He felt something soothe his mind, and a strong desire to sleep came over him. She took her hands away, shaking off a look of weariness, and smiled.

"Wash and rest now, Chip. You have earned it. Tomorrow, we will discuss preparation." She turned to the wizard, who tried to wave her away, but she was having none of it. The queen held his hands in a firm grip until he stopped resisting, and Chip saw her eyes blaze again. He realized how tired and dirty the wizard looked. Xander's face was etched with deep lines of weariness. The boy realized that the old man had not slept at all in the last two days. Even as he watched, the lines began to disappear, and his cuts mended until they were barely visible. She let go, and Chip saw a look of exhaustion cross her features, which she brushed off.

"Thank you," Xander said, bowing his head. Chip followed suit.

"Get a good night's sleep. You are safe here. We will talk tomorrow." She smiled wearily and departed. The wizard looked over at the boy. Both acknowledged the improvement in the other.

"She was one of the most gifted healers we had at the Guild," Xander said. "Few can match her skill. Charlotte has very little wizard fire for fighting as yellow is the lowest Level of Power, but it is well suited for healing."

Chip shook his head in wonder. "I had no idea she could use magic."

"She hides it well," the wizard agreed. "King Barton did not know either." Chip's eyes widened in amazement. "The rule in the Guild is to keep your magic a secret unless it's necessary. Just as vital is keeping secret your knowledge of another Guild member's magic. When challenged, the element of surprise can be as important as the magic itself. There is no sense in letting potential enemies know your strengths. For me and the other Higher Level Wizards, we choose to display it to force respect from our adversaries. It will make them think twice before crossing us. Only those of great strength should show their Power, but even then, at their discretion."

"When should I show my Power?" Chip whispered. The wizard leaned forward.

"You are the only one at the Demon King's Level, other than the Red-Eyed King in the Ancient City. The prophecy on the first page of *The Great Forget* book, subject to interpretation, states that knowledge of the Great Forget is attainable only when one red-eye remains. The Unnamed One will be looking to kill anyone with red eyes. He is much stronger now and likely wishes to enter the Ancient City again, this time to kill the Red-Eyed King. If he senses your Power, he will hunt you down and destroy you." The boy felt a sudden wave of fear and nodded in understanding.

"How can I possibly defeat him? He is at the Red Level and has absorbed the Power from many demon babies. He must be stronger than anyone," Chip declared with a heavy sigh.

Xander smiled. "I have learned through the ages that the Creator gives us the chance to balance. We still do not know your full strength. At any Level, there are great variances. We also do not know how much extra Power the Unnamed One has absorbed over the millennia through his dark arts. It is true that three thousand years ago, his Power was unmatched. Upon his return, he could very well triumph.

"I sense the Red-Eyed King has the answers we seek. I suspect he could have killed me in the Ancient City but instead asked that I bring you before him. It is of your choosing to seek him out. He may kill you or give you purpose. In any event, sleep now." On that note, the wizard got up, rested a hand on the boy's shoulder, and entered the door on the left.

Chip stared after him. He sat silently for a few moments, digesting everything, then got up and yawned. The boy walked through the right door and gasped at the beautifully adorned bedroom, featuring a sumptuous four-poster bed draped with patterned burgundy blankets. Dark wainscoting ran from floor to ceiling, and a large, thick throw rug covered the oak floor. In the corner stood a wooden tub filled with steaming hot water. Looking puzzled, he approached the tub and peered over the edge. The squire must have taken large round rocks from the simmering hearth on the side of the room to keep the water warm. Without even thinking, he disrobed and slid into the soothing water. A mix of heady herbs filled his nostrils as he laid back in utter bliss.

After a lengthy period, he used the herbal soap provided and, when clean, wrapped himself in the thick, soft bathrobe beside the tub. The boy walked slowly across the luscious carpet, letting the fibres brush between his toes, then fell on the bed and crawled under the burgundy blankets. Many thoughts competed for dominance in his head, but the deep well of sleep beckoned. Chip let the warm caress envelop him in a cocoon of calm and fell into a deep slumber.

The orphan awoke to the muted sounds of voices permeating the bedroom door. He felt more refreshed than he had in a long time. Throwing the covers off, Chip crossed to the curtained window and peered out. Bright daylight made him squint, and he realized it was close to lunchtime. He had slept half the day away! The window looked down on the training yard, and the boy could make out the weapons master barking orders to a large regiment of soldiers. The commander was preparing them for the coming assault.

Looking farther out, he could see the city proper surrounded by the outer wall. He felt a pang of sadness for what was about to happen to the beautiful Kingdom of Vanalon. He raised his gaze to the twin peaks cradling the fabled Pass of Death.

The boy's eyes narrowed. The enemy would come from there, all teeth and claws. Unlimited variations of demons were about to descend upon his beautiful homeland, destroying everything in their path. A surge of anger rushed through his body, and the Wall appeared in his mind. All he had to do was push through and use his Power to destroy them. Yet the wizard had warned him not to, and he quelled his anger, thinking instead of finding Chase.

He turned to put on his clothes and realized how filthy they were. He decided instead to see who was conversing in the living room.

Again, he let the thick carpet squish through his toes as he crossed the room and opened the door. Chip could not help but smile.

Princess Eleanor and Chase were seated in the two living room chairs. Xander was standing in front of them, telling a story. They all looked up as the door opened, and Eleanor leapt up with a squeal. She ran across the room and gave him a mighty hug. He laughed and returned the embrace, feeling only slightly embarrassed at being in his bathrobe.

His best friend followed close behind and embraced him in a great bear hug. When Chip was finally set down, he could breathe again and began talking in a rush. They all had the same idea and tried to speak over one another until no one could understand anyone. After several moments, they all broke out laughing. The wizard rolled his eyes. Princess Eleanor took charge by dragging him to the living room chair. He sat down, trying to keep a straight face.

"Tell us what happened. We will be quiet." She looked at Chase, who nodded. They both squeezed into the other chair and waited for him to begin. Xander leaned against the mantle with an amused look. Chip paused, drew a deep breath, and recounted everything. Well, almost everything.

When the boy reached the part where he lit the signal fire and drew his sword to battle the ring of demons, Xander coughed and interjected, "The weapons master and I flew in to see Chip battling the demons, including their Dark Elf captain, with only his sword!" the wizard exclaimed with a flourish. "He took out several demons singlehandedly, but alas, there were too many. The weapons master and I arrived in time to assist our brave hero. Together, we killed the entire horde." He paused, deciding whether he had made his point, then nodded. "Carry on."

Chip knew Xander had interjected to remind him not to reveal his use of magic. The boy had already made a conscious, albeit frustrating, effort to refrain from mentioning his Power. He did not see why his two closest friends could not know but respected the wizard's advice. Besides, he had given his word, and to him, that was everything.

Chip continued telling the story, watching their jaws drop when he described the Dark Inner Circle Elf Elohan and the lightning bolt.

The princess wrung her hands when he described their fall into the churning river and how close he came to going over the High Falls. When he finished, they sat in stunned silence. Chase had a look of envy and pride on his face. Eleanor was staring at him in an odd way as if seeing him for the first time. Chip felt a little self-conscious, realizing he was still in his bathrobe. He rose to get dressed.

"Fresh clothes are by the door," Xander called, motioning towards a thatched basket of folded garments. Chip tried to hide his surprise but failed and, with a grin, picked up the basket. He went back to the bedroom to change. His old, tattered clothes were still in a dirty heap by the tub. The boy put on dark, finely woven breeches and a ruffled white tunic usually worn by those of nobility. In the bottom of the basket were soft, black leather boots that fit perfectly.

The boy returned to the living room to find Chase and Eleanor barraging the wizard with questions. Xander was trying to answer, but another question popped out before he could finish. Eleanor looked over first and inhaled sharply when she saw him dressed in fine clothes. She had that strange look again, which generated a mix of emotions. He smiled.

"Ah, there you are," the wizard said, turning away from the other two, trying to hide his relief but failing. "Why don't the three of you run off? We can meet in the council chambers at the start of the hour." The friends looked at each other and nodded as one.

"Let me take you through the rest of the palace." The princess grabbed their hands and yanked them out the door. "I have always wanted to show you certain sections." They took off down the hall, listening to her excited chatter. She took them through wing after wing, explaining each room's function, sometimes adding a story of her and Rupert growing up. They avoided the king's chambers, but then with a finger to her lips, the princess entered the empty throne room through a back door. Eleanor said one of Rupert's first commands was to prohibit access, but she didn't care. The room was cavernous, and when she talked, her voice had a distinct echo. When they stood before the throne, the princess laughed and sat herself upon it, pretending to issue commands. Chip and Chase both giggled into their hands.

Sounds of muffled talking reached them, and they all froze. Eleanor jumped off the throne to scurry under the huge dining table in the middle of the room. She frantically motioned for them to follow, and they just managed to duck under before someone entered. The three crawled on hands and knees to hide under the center of the enormous table.

They all heard the heavy throne room doors open, and someone announced, "King Rupert, may I start a fire for warmth?"

Chase's breath caught, and he mouthed to them. "That's my father."

They both nodded as Eleanor suppressed a laugh. Mr. Longfellow had been the squire for many years, so she easily recognized his voice.

"Yes, there is a chill in the air. Make it snappy, as I have a council meeting shortly," Rupert replied. The princess made a face at her brother's voice. The sounds of several other people entering the room startled them. Who was with Rupert?

Suddenly, chairs pulled out on either side, and three bodies plopped down. One person stretched out and crossed his legs. His toes almost touched Chip's face. He tried not to move, but a foul odour immediately filled his nose, which wrinkled on its own. He dared not make a sound.

"Bring us some food, squire," Rupert commanded. The king sat at the end of the table. Chase's face darkened at the tone he was using with his father. "You hungry, Biff?" The person with the smelly feet answered yes. "Chubs? Gunter?" The two on Eleanor's side both grunted in the affirmative. Chip could not believe that all three of Rupert's bully friends turned soldiers were right beside them. There were some bustling sounds, and light filled the room from the newly lit fire, extending shadows under the table.

"I will be back shortly with the food, My King," Chase's father said humbly and departed the throne room.

"Never liked that guy," Rupert said, spitting off to the side, "reminds me of Chase." The others chuckled. "Lucky I didn't tell the wizard that Chase is also going on kitchen duty for the rest of his life." The three bullies broke out into loud guffaws.

"That would have really pissed off the old fart," laughed Biff, slapping his knee. His smelly foot pulled back with the motion, allowing Chip to breathe again.

"Who does the wizard think he is, anyway?" The voice came from Eleanor's right, which meant Chubs. "You are the king. He has no right to order you around like that. Say the word, and I'll put him in his place."

"Ya, me too," the slow-witted Gunter added, scratching between his legs. The princess made a face and imitated a throwing-up motion. Chip and Chase tried not to laugh.

"You buffoons," Rupert raised his voice, "if I could, I would. However, if only one-tenth of the stories are true about that wily wizard, he is not to be trifled with. My father could put most men in their place, but Xander terrified him. Uncle Dominor told Barton many stories about the wizard when he was a boy that scared respect into him. Besides, if these demon tales are true, we can use the old man."

"What about Chip?" grumbled Biff, extending his legs again. This time, the tip of his boot hit the orphan in the nose. Biff's leg froze, and the boy moved his face right next to Eleanor's until their cheeks touched. The foot lifted up and down to see what it had hit but then, encountering nothing, settled back down. Chip felt sandwiched between a smelly foot odour on one side and a heady perfume smell from the princess. He could feel her laughing silently with their cheeks touching. For a crazy moment, he almost laughed aloud.

"Can't we just let Miss Stern have him?" Biff snorted. "I would love to see the orphan slave over every meal brought to us by Chase's father, whatever his name is." The others guffawed again.

"Isn't Squire his name?" asked Gunter. The others laughed even harder. Chip heard Chase's knuckles clench into fists. He could not turn around with his face pressed against the princess, but he waved his finger behind him, saying no.

"I want all of you to attend the council meeting," said Rupert when the laughter died, "In case I need assistance. Do not act like guards though. And you better stop staring at Eleanor, Chubs," he said darkly. "She's my sister." Chip felt her stiffen beside him.

"I thought she was looking at me, is all," Chubs said apologetically. "You know I would never do anything like that." He squirmed and extended his legs. Chip turned to see the bully's feet getting closer to the princess. They stopped next to her face, and now he smelled an odour from both sides. He turned towards Eleanor's face, and she did the same until their lips touched. They both froze, and she let out a small laugh.

Right before she did, Rupert spoke. "I want to know ..."

"What was that?" asked Gunter in his deep, slow voice.

"What was what?" asked Rupert, clearly irritated by the interruption.

"I thought I heard something."

They all paused. The princess pressed her lips against his. She then slowly moved them to his ear. "Shhh," she said. The touch tickled him, and he almost turned his face back into the smelly feet. There was an agonizing pause. Her lips felt good, but Chip was incredibly ticklish and tried his best to stifle a giggle. He was positive they were going to look under the table.

"Never mind," Gunter said.

"Anyways," Rupert continued with an annoyed edge, "why does the wizard take such an interest in Chip?"

The princess finally turned forward, dragging her lips across his cheek again. He felt a flush of warmth, then a pang of disappointment when she moved. *At least the tickling went away*, he thought. He tried to focus on the conversation since they were talking about him, but his thoughts were somehow jumbled.

The king continued, "Ever since he was a baby, my mother defended the little demon. When Miss Stern finally caught him turning his eyes red, the wizard stopped my father from throwing him to the wolves. Instead, they trained him to be even more dangerous. Now they worship him for lighting the signal fire and killing a couple of demons." He leaned forward conspiratorially. "What if he has been working with the demons all along, and his purpose was to let them through the barrier? What if the wizard is in on it?"

Gunter let out a long fart. Biff belched at the same time, wiggling his feet. Chip almost gagged. Chase muttered a curse and then started making small, strangling noises after inhaling Gunter's gas.

"You are probably right," Chubs said. "I never thought of that."

"What's that sound?" Gunter asked. Chase was letting out faint whimpering noises, trying not to suffocate.

At that moment, the doors to the throne room opened, and the squire's voice proclaimed, "My King, your meal is ready."

"It's about time," Rupert responded, ignoring the others. "Bring it quick. We must go to a meeting." They could hear the squire shuffling over and setting something heavy down on the table. Smells of sizzling meat, steamed vegetables, and spices wafted through the air. "Where are the cakes and pastries?"

"I'm sorry, King Rupert," Chase's father said. "I was going to bring those after."

"Ah, too late now. We are in a rush. Next time, do not make that mistake. Eat up, boys."

They heard the squire's footsteps recede as he apologized again and left the room. The next while involved noisy sounds of eating, belching, and clanging dishes. A chicken leg fell from what must have been Biff's meaty hand and rolled across the floor towards Chip. Both the boy and the princess inhaled sharply. Biff reached down to find the piece, but it had moved out of reach. Quick as thought, Chip grabbed the chicken leg and pushed it into Biff's probing, chubby fingers. The bully was half leaning over the chair's armrest as he reached, and for a second, his face appeared below the top of the table. Luckily, Biff's eyes focused only on the chicken leg, which he grabbed with a satisfied grunt before sitting up.

"Still good," he beamed and continued eating the leg, chewing loudly. Eleanor had a disgusted look on her face. Chip tried not to laugh. The talk continued about the food, and then Rupert's chair shot backwards.

"We are going to be late! Leave it for the help to clean up." He noisily drank something, and then a heavy goblet landed on the table, followed by a loud belch. The others pushed out their chairs at the same time.

Chip felt a sense of relief that they were leaving. The group did not even bother pushing their chairs in. Gunter stood last and bent over to adjust his pant leg. They could all see the back of his large, greasy head. He tried to get up with a wheeze, but Gunter's head hit the top of the table, and he fell forward on all fours between Chase and Eleanor. They all froze, knowing the gambit was up. Gunter cursed and pushed himself backwards with eyes closed in pain. All he had to do was open them and see them clear as day.

Instead, he shuffled backwards with a wince and then pushed off the ground with his greasy hands. Gunter's eyes opened as he straightened just as the lip of the table blocked his view. He paused momentarily while the others laughed at his antics, then turned and lumbered after them. After a few moments, they heard the door close, and the throne room was silent.

In a flash, they were out from under the table, laughing hard and holding their stomachs. Then the throne doors opened, and the laughter died in their throats. Chase's father stood in the doorway with a shocked look. They waved him forward, and to their relief, he was alone.

"My princess," he said, bowing low. "What are you doing in here?" He gave Chase a disapproving look.

"It's alright, Dad. The princess was showing us around." Chase grinned.

"Oh, were you talking to Rupert and his friends?" he asked, puzzled.

"No, it seems we missed them." Chase smiled innocently.

The squire looked at the size of the throne room with a calculating expression. Obviously, he was wondering how they could have reached the center table without bumping into King Rupert, who had left moments before.

"The king has commanded that access to the throne room only be granted with his permission," he said with a polite expression.

"I must have forgotten," the princess said smoothly. "Let's not stress my brother out by telling him we were here." The squire nodded and tried not to smile.

"Of course, My Princess. As you wish." He bowed again.

"We've got to go, Dad. We're going to a council meeting." His father looked at the tall boy proudly. "We will go out the back if that's alright."

"Yes," Eleanor concurred. "Thank you, Mr. Longfellow." Chase's dad bowed low, hiding his smile.

The trio rushed through the door at the back of the throne room, giggling with excitement over their close call. They started talking over each other. The princess led them down several halls until they arrived in front of two tall wooden doors with gold knobs.

She turned and looked the boys up and down to make sure they were presentable. Her eyes stopped at Chip's neck, and she adjusted his collar before proceeding. She looked different to him now, or perhaps he was different. Either way, it felt exciting to him. The princess gave him one final smile then turned and opened the doors.

3

"You're late," King Rupert said coldly. "Take your seats."

A large, extravagant table surrounded by plush, high-backed red velvet chairs filled most of the room. Seated at the head of the table was the king, with the queen on one side and an empty chair on his other, presumably for the princess. Xander sat in the next seat, followed by the weapons master and the Captain of the Guard, Mack. Behind the king stood Biff, Chubs, and Gunter. The princess motioned for the boys to sit beside the queen while she filled the empty seat next to Rupert.

"Our apologies. I had to use the bath, if you must know. Greetings, Mother." She acknowledged the wizard and soldiers. "Carry on."

"I would hear what our wise wizard has to say," said Rupert. "Messenger pigeons are flying as we speak to Toron, the Wizard's Guild, and our closest ally, Calgar. Up to one thousand Calgarian soldiers should arrive in one week to make us twelve hundred strong. At that point, we may even be powerful enough to repel these pesky demons ourselves. What do you think, Xander?"

The wizard studied the king with an unreadable expression. Calmly, he said, "I want you to imagine the vast plains to the east of Calgar when you come out of the mountains. You can see leagues in every direction. Now imagine it filled with an army of creatures screaming for human blood. Many have long teeth and claws that can slice a man into pieces in the blink of an eye. Three millennia ago, the demons filled the plains before us as far as the eye could see. What organizes these creatures is a group of Dark Elves commanded by an Inner Circle of their eleven most powerful mages. Controlling them all is General Morgo. He is a fearsome, soulless creature mired in the Dark Arts. No one even knows from what race he descends as his form varies.

"All of them are commanded by the Unnamed One, King of the Dark Elves, and King of the Demons. His Power is beyond anything we have ever known. We defeated him with the aid of the Orb of Power found long ago in an ancient city. Even its Power, in combination with all the great wizards of old, the Light Elves, and the trolls and dwarves, was still not strong enough to kill the Unnamed One and his Inner Circle. However, it did drive them backwards through the mountains until, finally, their backs were to the ocean. The Demon King built rafts and fled with his army across a narrow expanse of water to a large island off the coast. It was once called Victory Island, filled with happy, loving people. The demons killed and consumed the entire population, taking it for their own. It is now Demon Island.

"The Wizard Guild and the Light Elves did not want to risk crossing the coastal waters to continue the Great Battle, so they used all their remaining Power to create a barrier around the island. It was the greatest feat of magic ever produced by the combined races, aided in great part by the Orb of Power. For three thousand years, the barrier stood, imprisoning the Unnamed One, but he has grown stronger. It will not contain him much longer. A few days ago, after our battle in the Pass of Death, I travelled across the beach, now called the Desolate Plain, to examine the barrier. I sensed weakness in it at certain spots, but it was not just from a failure of the Power that built it. No, I am afraid a force from within is weakening it, a force even greater than the barrier."

There was an ominous silence as he let the words sink in.

"The Unnamed One is inexorably destroying it," the wizard continued. "He has grown strong, consuming Power through unspeakable means. It is only a matter of time before the entire barrier collapses. Meanwhile, he can allow dozens through, which will grow to hundreds, then thousands, and finally, all of them. So, King Rupert, I appreciate that you would like to resolve this with twelve hundred men, but I am afraid all we can hope is to stall their advance."

Everyone was silent in the council room. The king sat stone-faced, grappling with the enormity of the wizard's grim prediction. The queen looked at him compassionately and laid a comforting hand on his.

The king pulled his hand back and looked hard at the old man. "There must be some way to defeat them. We did it before. Where is this Orb of Power? Let's use it again and rebuild the barrier."

Xander sighed. "The orb is lost."

There was a moment of shocked silence. Rupert was speechless.

"How is that possible?" the king finally managed.

"After the Great Battle, King Luminor of the Light Elves picked up the orb for safekeeping. Shortly thereafter, the Light Elves and the Orb of Power disappeared."

"Well… Surely someone can find them," stammered the king. "Use your magic or something."

The wizard smiled, but no mirth showed in his eyes. "I have tried. My brother Balor and I have spent much time searching for the lost Light Elves. Their homeland is far to the northeast in Lavralor, named after their first king. It is an enormous island facing the vast Eastern Ocean. There resided Elvar, the city of the Light Elves. It was one of the wonders of the world. White towers sparkled pristinely amidst the snow and ice. In the short summer, the surrounding ancient trees created a green oasis overlooking the endless blue ocean. Great Councils of the Races were held in its glorious white halls. There were even peace talks between the trolls, dwarves, and elves.

"After the Breaking, when the Dark Elves split from the Light, a shadow fell over the world. The Unnamed One grew in power and spawned his demon army. He settled far to the west in these very mountains. For centuries, they fought. These were the Elf Wars. The Demon King, looking for an advantage, learned there was an ancient city of great magic that none could enter."

Chip nodded, remembering the story. It was being retold for the king's benefit.

"The Unnamed One defeated a powerful guardian to gain access to the city, and there he found the orb. In doing so, he awoke an ancient Power but managed to escape to his demon spawning grounds. From there, he launched his entire might at the races. In the Great Battle on the plains, he was prepared to defeat the combined strength of the old wizards and the Light Elves. The armies of men, dwarves, and trolls all came to lend aid. Even with that strong alliance, we knew we were not strong enough to fight the Dark Elves, the demon army, and the Orb of Power.

"In response, we hatched a daring plan the night before the Great Battle. I stole the orb from the demon's encampment, and we used it to drive the Demon King to the Western Ocean. He escaped to Demon Island, and we raised the barrier to contain him. The Light Elves took the orb as compensation for the many losses they had suffered and endured over the centuries fighting the Dark Elves. My brother Balor protested, causing hostility and division. When he declared himself High Wizard, the Light Elves withdrew from the Great Council. They retreated to their homeland and disappeared without a trace."

The king looked incredulous. The rest of the council remained quiet. Chase shook his head in wonder while Eleanor seemed lost in thought. The weapons master remained impassive as ever.

"So, the tales are true," Rupert finally said. "You stole the Orb of Power right out from under the nose of the Demon King." He seemed impressed. "Is there any way to find the lost Light Elves?"

"From what my brother and I could gather, the Light Elves used great magic on themselves. Its residue permeates what was once Elvar. The entire city is gone."

"What do you mean gone?" the king asked in bewilderment.

"I mean gone without a trace. We believe they used the orb to make it disappear."

"So is it still there?" pressed the king.

"No, I'm afraid not. It is not hidden. It has simply vanished."

There was a long pause. Rupert finally threw up his hands. "So what do we do now?"

Xander cleared his throat. "We must convene the High Council in Toron. There has not been a meeting for three millennia. Send messages to the different races. High Wizard Balor and High King Dominor will preside over this most vital of meetings. From there, we will determine how to slow the advancing demon army. Before this, we must find the Light Elves. Without the Orb of Power, we do not stand a chance. The great wizards of old are gone. The Guild is weaker than ever.

"The orb can only increase the strength of its users. In a non-magic wielder's hands, it is useless. In a weak user, it can make them strong. In a powerful wizard, it can give great Power. Unfortunately, we now have less to start with than the days of old. Worse, the Demon King has grown stronger." He paused, glancing at Chip. "Yet the Creator may provide balance in the days to come. If not, the age of humans is at an end."

Xander let out a long sigh that spoke of great sacrifice over countless years. "I have stayed vigilant in anticipation of this day. My duty is to protect the races using what the Creator has provided. A dark, long shadow is coming, worse than anything we have ever experienced. I did not tell anyone what I saw through the barrier on the Desolate Plain. I used my Power to reach through a rift to get a sense of what is on the other side."

He stopped, and Chip saw true fear in the wizard's eyes.

"He is stronger than I could imagine. The Demon King sensed me and turned. In that instant, he recognized me as the one who stole his orb millennia ago. He let out a howl of rage and threw his Power at me. I barely withdrew in time to pull the gap closed, but his strength buckled the entire barrier. He was mighty in the days of old, but now..." The wizard shook his head.

"What if the orb is not enough?" asked Princess Eleanor in a small voice. There was a long pause.

"Then we fall defending the Light." The wizard looked at her with sad eyes. "Sometimes we lose, despite everything we do. All I know is nothing is permanent, not even darkness. A great evil is coming, and things will never be the same. All we hold dear may indeed be lost. Several of the great wizards of old gave their very spirit essences to create the barrier. That means they gave their souls and ceased to exist." A look of unimaginable pain crossed his face. "My father, High Wizard Arkan, was one of them."

Chip looked up in shock. Arkan was the powerful wizard who could not defeat the guardian of the Ancient City.

Xander looked down. "He gave up any hope of existence in this life or the next to contain the Unnamed One. I will never know him again. My father's sacrifice gave us three thousand years of peace. Now it is failing." The council was silent.

"There is still hope," Chip said softly. They all turned. "The demons are worse than anything I have ever imagined, but everything has a weakness." The weapons master nodded approvingly. "We must find something stronger than the orb."

"Nothing is stronger than the Orb of Power," King Rupert sneered. "Everybody knows that." Chip looked embarrassed but defiant.

"There may be something else," the wizard said solemnly. "Something hidden in the Ancient City where the orb was found. The problem is retrieving it might not be survivable."

"Why not?" asked the king.

"There is still a being of even greater Power than the one that used to guard the entrance. This one sleeps but awakens if you trespass or try to take something. He is the Red-Eyed King. Even the Unnamed One fled from him. He may have answers that can save us... or destroy us. If we approach him with the orb, perhaps we can force him to give us those answers."

"So, to be clear," Chase jumped in, "we have no chance right now of defeating a monstrous army led by a Demon King so powerful that weak people can die just by gazing at him, but we may be able to stop him if we find a lost Orb of Power held by the Light Elves, who are also lost, and then if we find this orb we only need to enter the Ancient City to confront an entity previously more powerful than the Unnamed One, and then use the orb to make this entity give us answers or objects of Power that may or may not help us defeat this Demon King who has had three thousand years to get stronger, or else we all die, right?"

He leaned back, self-satisfied.

"Exactly!" Xander said in approval, unable to hold back a smile. Eleanor giggled.

The king sat back with a look of helplessness, "Dear Creator," he moaned.

The queen patted his hand. "Now, now, Rupert. Difficult things usually look impossible at the beginning. Chip is right. There is always hope."

"That's right. The odds may not quite be in our favour, but there is still a chance," the wizard said, trying to sound reassuring given the almost impossible probabilities. "Perhaps the High Council will come up with a better plan." He smiled weakly at them, not sounding very convincing.

"If I may," said the weapons master. All eyes turned to hear the ordinarily silent high commander. "I do not pretend to have all the answers to defeat this foe, but I know how best to defend against their initial attack and allow reinforcements to arrive. Captain Mack and I have issued orders to dig trenches and spike pits around the walls to slow the demons. This will enable our archers to pick them off as they struggle. The soldiers will have barrels of pitch ready on top of the walls to drench and ignite the creatures as they climb. If the gates get breached, we fall back to the main square behind a self-made barrier to slow their advance to the palace.

"I recommend creating a covered moat outside the castle's walls filled with spikes. If the palace gates get breached, we fall back to the keep. Upon fail, we must make arrangements to escape the palace, preferably in secret. We then head for the City of Calgar to stage a secondary defence. When and if Calgar falls, our remaining army will retreat across the plains to Toron.

"In the meantime, we must reach the capital for the High Council meeting, which should be set for ninety days hence. That should give us enough time for the races to convene and for us to find the orb. All the citizens and villagers of Vanalon should begin journeying to Calgar. Other than the soldiers, the city must be deserted before the first attack."

"How do you propose we secretly exit the palace?" the king asked, trying not to sound desperate. Garth Stone did not answer. The queen looked around.

"I would ask that your three personal guards leave the room, please." She looked straight at Rupert, indicating it was not a debate. The king waved his hand, motioning for them to leave. Biff and Chubs rolled their eyes in annoyance and left while Gunter followed with a confused look. Queen Charlotte waited until they were gone.

"There is a secret passage to escape the palace," she revealed. "It leads east somewhere by the One Road. Only a few know of its existence. They are sitting in this room, except for one other." She turned to Chase. "Your father is the other."

The king looked angry. "Why does a squire know something before me?" he fumed.

"You have only been king a couple of days. I am telling you now. The squire knows because he has given us years of loyal service, and we need someone else to know the location if we fall." The king grumbled but conceded the logic of her response. Chase beamed with pride for his father.

"I will be there to defend you if the palace falls," the weapons master said to the king. "We have much to do. I will send small scouting parties to monitor the demons' activities while we prepare. I may have to change tactics at a moment's notice. With only two hundred men, we must pray that the demons do not attack until reinforcements arrive. May I ask leave to make the necessary preparations to fortify Vanalon?"

King Rupert looked around, then nodded. Captain Mack also rose with his commander. They saluted at the same time and took their leave.

Rupert looked nervous. The full scope of the invasion was weighing on him. Xander looked at the inexperienced monarch and spoke words of consolation. "You are not alone in this. We are here to help. My magic provides a formidable defence against this attack. It will not be easy for them to take Vanalon. However, when reinforcements arrive, I must take leave. Going with me will be my Protector." The king looked mortified. The wizard shook his head and smiled. "Do not fear. The reinforcements will have several wizards of good strength and hardy soldiers. Their captain is experienced. My tasks are critical. I must, among other things, find this lost orb. Oh, lest I forget, I will also be taking Chip and Chase."

"Why!?" Eleanor blurted out before even the king could speak. "I thought we would escape together." Rupert seemed irritated but awaited the answer. The wizard nodded as if expecting the question.

"The four of us will be journeying to find the Light Elves and the Orb of Power. We must move swiftly to obtain this talisman before the High Council meeting. Chase is nearly as adept as Garth with the sword, and Chip is not far behind. I need a small, skilled party who can move quickly to complete this mission. It will be very dangerous. If all goes well, we will convene in ninety days in Toron. We are with you every step of the way until reinforcements arrive. I am confident we can repel a sizable preliminary demon force on our own. I also ask for a larger three-bedroom guest suite, so Chase can join us. I want their input to help plan our next steps. It will make meetings easier if we reside in the palace. With your leave, King Rupert, I would like to adjourn the meeting. We have much to do."

The king was about to ask more questions, especially about Chase and Chip, then seemed to think better of it. With a slight glower, he nodded. The two boys rose with the wizard, bowed awkwardly, then moved to the door. Chip glanced backward to see the princess staring at him with a look of concern and something else. He vowed to keep her safe no matter what happened.

Over the next week, the boys, under the weapons master's guidance, helped prepare and secure Vanalon. Many townspeople and villagers were recruited to dig trenches. Soldiers went to outlying homes and villages, asking all residents to pack their belongings and take the One Road to safety. King Henry of Calgar was a fair monarch who would welcome them in their time of need. His city was much larger, boasting over five thousand defenders. Up to one thousand of those were set to arrive in Vanalon within the week.

At regular intervals, Garth Stone sent small scouting parties to assess the demon's movements. For the first few days, there was no sight of them. The patrols ventured as far as the Rocky River, reporting that the bridge was still down. They detected no movement on the other side but described smoke rising from base camp. A dark cloud seemed to cover the two peaks. It was unknowable whether it was the Dark Elf Elohan's work or simply a coincidence. More ominous, strange green flashes started appearing in the Pass of Death.

Several more days went by, and then reports of missing villagers surfaced. Some inhabitants refused to believe demons existed and chose to remain in their homes. Spine-chilling screams were reported at night, especially from some outlying houses. When the other villagers investigated in the morning, they often found human remains scattered inside the dwelling. Sometimes, the owners had vanished without a trace. These reports convinced many other residents to abandon their homes and head for Calgar. Still, some were steadfast and stayed on, certain it was a pack of mountain wolves or rabid animals.

At the end of the third day, a small scouting party led by a lead scout named Cooper rushed up to the weapons master in the yard. The boys were close by and heard the conversation.

"A sizable force of demons are building a bridge on the Rocky River," Cooper reported, face flushed. "They seem to be following instructions from a robed Dark Elf."

"What colour was his robe?" asked Garth.

"Dark brown," answered the scout. The weapons master nodded.

"It must be Elohan."

"This Elohan saw us." Cooper gulped. "There is a perpetual cloud over him. He raised his hands and... threw a storm our way, though we were quite distant. We tried to flee, but a force of wind and rain slammed into us, knocking the horses over. Craig was crushed by his horse, and Jero was impaled on a tree. We managed to scramble further into the forest to safety."

Garth sighed, shaking his head. "Send condolences to the soldiers' families. How many demons and Dark Elves did you count?"

The scout paused in thought. "I would say about one hundred demons." He looked fearful. "Some were huge, like immense bears, and carried logs strapped to their backs."

The commander considered that. "Send out rotating scouting parties so we always have eyes on them, but stay as far away as possible. Elohan's Power will lessen with distance, so you should be safe. Even so, be vigilant. I need to know when they complete the bridge." The soldier saluted and left.

Chip walked up to the weapons master as he contemplated the new information.

"How can the demons look so different?" the boy inquired.

"The Dark Elves breed the demons for various tasks," Garth explained. If you keep mating large ones together over a long period of time, they get bigger. Some are bred small so they can move in stealth, others are crafted for battle, and some, it seems, are made for heavy lifting. They had three millennia to design an army perfectly suited for war and destruction. None are magic wielders, so in that aspect, we are safe. The Dark Elves are another story. The strongest are the Inner Circle of Eleven and General Morgo."

"Why do all elves have the Power," Chip asked curiously. Chase sidled next to him to hear the answer.

The commander looked over and smiled. "Questions are how we learn. The elves go back to the Great Forget. They are few in number, but all are magic wielders, unlike humans. We do not know why. The eye colour of an elf tells us what Level of Power they hold, even when they are not using magic. With humans, the eyes can be a different colour from their magic. Only a small number of humans have access to the Power. Again, we do not know why. The Dark Elves have black eyes from abuse of the Power due to the permanent removal of their Walls. Their Level is only revealed when they use magic. Most of the ones commanding the demon hordes are Greens, with the Higher Levels forming the Inner Circle. The Yellows were weaker, and most died out during the Elf Wars.

"All races we know of go back to the Great Forget. Humankind, being the most numerous, arrogantly assumes they are the original race. They want control over the others. The elves, comprised of only magic wielders, feel they are the superior race. Magic wielding humans who pass the Guild's Trials are called wizards, whereas all elves, dwarves, and trolls with the Power are considered mages. Wizards and mages have fought great contests and duels over the millennia." He leaned towards them conspiratorially. "The elves usually win." The boys laughed.

"How does someone become a Protector?" Chase asked.

Garth turned to the tall boy. "Higher Level wizards may be assigned Protectors. The land's greatest warriors come to train and fight in the Wizard's Guild, learning to be Protectors. They must pass Tests to be Certified."

"What about Xander," Chip asked. "Where does he rank?"

"He may be the most powerful wizard in the world, save for his older brother, High Wizard Balor," Garth answered. "Their father, Arkan, was considered the greatest of all wizards. He was instrumental in the Great Battle and gave the ultimate sacrifice. All of them were Blue Level."

Chip hesitated, then asked, "Why did Arkan sacrifice himself?"

Garth paused before answering, "It is not for me to say. Giving up one's spirit essence is extremely rare and takes great sacrifice. Those who do it will never know what afterlife awaits us. Their soul becomes a weapon of immense Power and then ceases to exist. What I do know is that we need to honour his great sacrifice.

"Now, we have much to do. Take the training squad and finish building the blockade in the main square leading to the palace. We have less time than I thought. One hundred demons may not sound like a lot, but a single demon crafted perfectly for warfare can kill several men in the open. Thankfully, we have walls to fall back on." He smiled. "And, of course, a wizard."

He motioned them away and strode to Captain Mack to share the report.

The boys stood for a moment. "That's the most he's said in the last three months," Chase said.

They both laughed. Despite the gravity of the situation, Chip could not help but enjoy the moment. He could always count on his best friend to bring levity to anything. They looked at each other and rushed to follow the high commander's instructions.

That night, the scouting patrol on duty came back to report a rudimentary bridge made of whole trees now spanned the Rocky River. At ten trunks across, a horde of demons could make it over rapidly. The city reached high alert. A substantial demon force now had the means to reach Vanalon at any time. At most, the defenders would have half a day's notice.

The demons did not cross that night or the next. Reports, however, came in that the demon force on the other side of the river had now tripled. The good news was that the reinforcements from Calgar should be arriving any day.

The next morning's report was grave. It came at dawn from a guard manning the gates. The boys stood with the weapons master in the stable and listened to the message from the flustered man. Several small demons built for assassination had crept up behind the scouting party and killed three of the four men before they could react. The lone surviving soldier, Lead Scout Cooper, fought them off, but only after sustaining severe wounds.

He was now at the gates, draped over his mount, bleeding heavily. Garth ordered the boys to ready three horses from the stables.

They rode at a gallop down to the gates and found the wounded soldier lying against the city wall. The guardsmen had pressed cloths against several wounds, but their faces were grim. Garth leapt off his horse and crouched beside the man. He scanned the soldier's injuries, and a look crossed his features. It was apparent, even to the two boys, that the lead scout would not survive long. Chip recognized the man from two days earlier.

"What is your report, Cooper?" the weapons master asked him, crouching low.

The young soldier's breathing was laboured, and he looked afraid. "Commander, they came up behind us… in the night. We did not notice. They were so quiet. We were also distracted by the lights." Cooper said haltingly.

"What lights?" pressed Garth.

"The torches. There were so many," gasped Cooper. "At least five hundred. They started crossing the bridge, and then we were… attacked. The creatures were small but quick. There were four of them. One for each of us. The others died instantly. I turned as the one behind me stabbed and managed… to pull out my sword and kill it. The others surrounded me, darting in and out, stabbing. I ran to my horse." He looked up with fearful eyes. "They are coming… I don't want to die…" He choked, and a mouthful of blood ran over his lips. He tried to breathe in but could not. His face turned blue, and he looked at his commander with pleading eyes.

The weapons master leaned down and whispered, "Thank you for your service, Lead Scout Cooper. Your sacrifice will save many lives. Go in peace." The soldier stiffened, and his eyes glazed over. Chip felt a lump in his throat and turned away. Chase stared with mounting anger.

Garth Stone stood up, and a calm fury filled his eyes. He looked like a piece of chiselled granite. His black garb bristled with all manner of weapons.

Suddenly, a scream sounded from one of the guards on the wall.

"They are on the valley rim!"

4

The High Commander of Vanalon ran up the stairs two at a time to reach the top of the city wall and looked to where the agitated guard pointed. A dark mass was gathering at the top of the valley.

Garth cursed. "Sound the bells! All men to their posts. They will be upon us in less than three hours." He gathered several soldiers around him, including the two boys. "Take your horses to the nearest villages and tell anyone who has not evacuated to make for the city gates. They shut in two hours." He locked eyes with Chase and Chip. "You two stay together and do not go out far. If you see any sign of the enemy, race back."

They saluted, mounted their steeds, and took off through the gates. Chip wore his red cloak to ward off the chill as they rode. It had been mended after his Manhood Quest. He looked at his best friend and pointed to the right. Several small villages and single homes were nestled in the north part of the valley where the river bent behind the city. They reached the first village after a brisk gallop. It was only a small collection of quaint homes surrounding a trader's shop and local tavern. The hamlet looked empty except for a group of men standing outside the store.

"The demons are here!" Chip yelled as he reigned in his horse in front of the villagers. "Get to the city. The gates close in two hours." Two men nodded and hurried off. Three others in front of the tavern broke out in laughter.

A large, potbellied man with a long grey beard holding a beer tankard barked at them, "I've lived here me whole life. I ain't gunna let a couple of whelps like you tell me what I gunna do." He belched loudly while his two friends snickered. "Besides, there ain't no such thing as demons."

He waved them off and turned around, leaning on the rail.

Chase jumped off his horse and tied it to the rail. He pushed past the men and entered the tavern. The barkeep was busy pouring ale for two villagers at the counter. He was bald and short with a dirty apron.

"What can I get you, lads?" he asked after handing a full glass to one of his customers. A woman appeared from the kitchen behind him. Chip saw two small children playing on the floor in the room beyond. The doors to the tavern opened behind them, and the three men, including the one with the potbelly, sauntered in.

Chase did not turn but loudly beseeched the barkeep, "Sir, you must evacuate the village and take your family inside the city before the gates close. The demon army is at the top of the valley. You have less than two hours."

"We already told you runts that we ain't gunna go," the pot-bellied drunk called from behind them. Chip thought the word runt was strange, given that Chase was taller than all of them and muscled. Granted, they were young, but runts?

"I cannot just shut down my business and let someone rob the place." The barkeep shook his head.

"Jake, listen to them," the woman said. "If what they say is true, we need to protect the children." She gave her husband a pleading look, but he ignored her.

The men behind them moved closer.

"We asked you nicely to leave, but you ain't listening. Now we gunna throw you out." The drunk placed his empty beer on a table and turned to Chip. "I'm gunna start with you, little boy." He closed his meaty hand into a fist and swung it hard. Chip easily dodged, stepping to the side. He was about to counter when he saw a blur of motion as Chase moved in lightning-fast, landing a perfect right hook on the edge of the man's jaw. The pot-bellied man did not see it coming. There was a popping sound as his jaw dislocated, and he spun around, landing on his back, out cold.

The other two men sprang into action, coming at Chase from the left. Chip stepped forward to lend aid but realized it would not be necessary. Chase had already swung around with a lethal back fist that slammed into the second man's temple, knocking him out instantly. The tall boy continued with a right-turning kick that landed on the third man's sternum. It sent him flying into the wall, which he struck hard and slowly slid down, clutching his chest. Within moments, Chase had incapacitated all three.

Chip winced. "Was there any way to handle that differently?" he asked politely.

Chase looked at him with a blank expression. "No." He turned to the barkeep. "We are now giving you a direct order on behalf of the High Commander of Vanalon to take your family into the city. Rouse these men and go. Now!" Chase's tone brooked no argument. The barkeep looked once more at the three men on the ground, then nodded. "We will be coming back this way, and all of you better be gone," Chase added. The man's wife smiled in thanks.

The two boys left the tavern and went to the trading store, where several people were purchasing goods. This time, Chase was more direct. He ordered everyone to get into the city immediately on orders of the high commander, not taking no for an answer. Chip watched with an amused expression. One man tried to object, and Chase grabbed his tunic and threw him out the door. He then rested his hand on the pommel of his sword. The boy's size was intimidating, and his voice seemed to get deeper by the moment. That, coupled with a look of stone, seemed to do the trick. *He learned that from the weapons master*, thought Chip, trying not to smile.

When they cleared the first village, the boys proceeded to the following two with the same message. The few townspeople who resisted received a slap or a welt, which seemed to change their view. They were past the first hour and knew they had to turn back shortly.

Ahead of them were several remote houses that looked vacant. They were about to turn around when Chip spotted a small plume of smoke in the distance from one of the farthest houses. People were still in the home.

"There's smoke coming from that one," Chip indicated. "We are out of time, but I don't want to leave them."

"Neither do I," Chase agreed. "Let's go." They urged their horses into a gallop but had to slow down as they entered a forested area, and the path narrowed. The horses gingerly picked their way down the trail, meandering over rocks and tree roots. Finally, it ended in a wide cleared area where a small wooden house stood with a smoking chimney. A strange pall of silence seemed to hang over the clearing. Something did not feel right. The horses whinnied uneasily.

A sharp scream cut through the silence like a knife. Looking at each other, they kicked their horses' flanks and reigned up to the front door. Another scream, this time much deeper, joined the first one, and sounds of a physical struggle ensued. The cry of children intermingled with the others. Chase crashed through the front door first, followed by Chip. They burst into the main living area of the small home to witness a nightmare.

Three demons crouched in the middle of the room. A family of four huddled in the corner behind a makeshift barricade consisting of an overturned oak table and several stools. A burly man was trying to protect his wife and two small children from the creatures with a large two-sided axe. A long gash ran down his arm, dripping bright crimson blood. A dead demon was on the floor near the adjoining dining room. The man must have killed one before getting cornered by the others. The two small children, a boy and a girl, hid behind them. The girl was crying uncontrollably.

The demons whirled around at the sound of the door crashing open. One was squat with bulging muscles and long tusks jutting from a square face. Its legs were like tree trunks ending in flat, hairy feet. The other two were similar to the one Chip defeated on the bridge over the Rocky River. They were tall and slender with supple muscles and long limbs ending in razor-sharp claws. Rows of sharp fangs protruded from their gaping mouths. The demons stood naked with coarse tufts of hair covering various parts of their bodies.

The short, bull-necked demon lowered its head and charged at Chase. The two taller ones sprang to the sides. Hampered by the confines of the room, Chase drew his sword in one fluid motion and brought the hilt down full force on the charging demon's head. A loud hollow ring sounded as the thing's head cracked like a melon. The beast fell unmoving at his feet.

Without communicating, both boys spread out, each taking one of the two remaining demons. Chip pulled his sword in a smooth arc. The demons hissed warily at the shimmering elven blade. Both darted in simultaneously, trying to rake them with their sharp claws. The boys blocked the attacks using short motions of their swords as they had been taught to do in confined places. They knew not to risk broad swings, as the sword point could get stuck in the wall or ceiling, freezing their motion and inviting instant death from a skilled opponent. The weapons master had trained them in almost all scenarios over the years.

After parrying, they jabbed small, deep holes in their opponents with flicks of their swords. The demons backed up against the overturned table, oozing black blood from growing wounds. The man with the axe used a short two-handed swing to decapitate the one fighting Chase. Its body spasmed and fell to the floor with a thud. The remaining demon turned in all directions, hissing with hate and dripping blood on the floor.

"You will die," it croaked. The demon swung wildly at Chip, who sheared one of its claws off at the wrist. At the same time, Chase took off its left leg at the knee with a downward slice. The creature screamed and fell on its back. Writhing on the ground, it looked at the boys with its black, almond eyes. Incredibly, the thing laughed.

"We are many..." the demon intoned before its voice cut short as Chase's sword entered its mouth and emerged out the back of its head. He drew the blade out and calmly cleaned it before sheathing it.

Chip was amazed at how relaxed Chase was in battling his first demons. The tall boy was indeed a weapon forged by one of the greatest masters in the world.

"Are you alright?" Chip asked the man with the axe. He had a strong build, and light brown hair framed an honest, tanned face. "What are your names?"

"Yes, thank you for your aid. I am Farn. This is my wife Sally and our children, Han and Beth. My family was in prayer to the Creator when these creatures broke through the back. My wife and I never believed the stories about demons and such." He was shaking as he looked at the bodies of the dead creatures. He wiped his brow, turned to his family, and moved the table out of the way. The two small children jumped into his arms. "You were very brave," he said, eyes wet.

"I am Chip, and this is my friend Chase. We have direct orders from the High Commander of Vanalon to gather anyone outside the city. We must make for the gates at once. There is little time. A demon army is approaching as we speak. Do you have horses?"

"Only one out back in the barn. I hope those creatures didn't kill it."

"Please go and saddle the horse. You ride with your wife. Chase and I will take the children." He motioned for the family to come outside. Chase followed Farn to the barn to ensure the horse was alive. Chip stood outside with Sally and the two children. The mother had long brown hair and a caring face that looked compassionately at her offspring. The girl had stopped crying but appeared understandably shaken. Her older brother, surprisingly, seemed calm.

Chip knelt in front of Han and Beth. The boy looked about seven years old, and his younger sister was five or six. "You are safe now," he said reassuringly. "We are going for a fast horse ride. If we see more black creatures, my friend and I will protect you. Your mother and father will ride their horse, and you will ride with us, alright?" They nodded solemnly, and the girl looked at her mother.

"It's fine. They are here to help us." Sally smiled despite her fear.

Chip could tell she was a good mother. Farn and Chase appeared with the family horse, which had survived. It looked old but able to carry its weight.

"Mount fast. We heard strange sounds in the forest at the back. Something is coming," Chase warned.

Chip looked around warily. A wind came from nowhere, and he noticed dark clouds moving into the valley. Chase picked up Beth, placed her on his horse, and leapt behind her. She looked absurdly small in front of his large frame. Chip did the same with the little boy, Han. Farn sat on the family horse with his wife behind him. A soft mewling sounded behind the house. They urged the horses across the clearing and onto the forested path.

Their mounts could only move at a quick walk as the path twisted and turned over the rocks and roots. It felt agonizingly slow. They heard a door bang and sounds of breaking furniture coming from the dwelling behind them, putting everyone on edge. The demons had found the home.

The small party continued along the winding path. Screams erupted behind them, which meant the demons had found their trail. The sounds of branches cracking in the distance confirmed their fears. They were able to push the horses into a trot as the path widened. The sounds of pursuit intensified until they could hear a cacophony of mewls and shrieks growing louder behind them.

Chip turned to see momentary glimpses of dark figures through the brush. Beth started crying again at the sounds. When it felt like the demons were upon them, they broke through the trees and kicked the horses into a full gallop. The path widened into the road leading to the village. Chip looked behind at the forest just as a small demon horde broke through. There were several short, stout ones with horns charging alongside tall, skinny, elongated demons. In the middle was a vicious-looking beast with long teeth and claws.

The horses galloped hard, urged on by fear of the creatures behind them. They gained distance on the short demons, but the elongated ones were catching up with their incredible strides. These had long necks and pointy heads with black almond eyes prominent on their triangular faces. Their mouths looked small until they opened them to let out spine-tingling shrieks, displaying double rows of sharp, pointed teeth. Fastest of all was the lone teeth and clawed demon. It was catching up with ease and would be upon them in moments.

"Chase!" warned Chip, pointing behind him. Farn and his wife were the slowest, being double mounted on an older horse. The boys slowed down to keep pace with them while pulling their swords. Without waiting for the others, the teeth and clawed demon leapt the last few paces and swung a claw to hamstring the lagging horse. Chip tried to swing down in time but was too far away. Luckily, Chase was able to reach it from the other side. Leaning low, he neatly sliced off its clawed hand, causing the thing to scream and stumble. The creature went down in a flurry of limbs but managed to roll to its feet. Two of the taller demons crashed into it from behind until they all rolled in a tangled knot of grey, twisted limbs.

An elongated one moved nimbly around the heap of bodies and came at Chip from an angle. It let out a mewl, which turned into a high-pitched shriek as it pushed off the ground with both long legs, turning itself into a living projectile. Chip pulled up on the reigns hard, causing the demon to land and stumble in front of his mount. He then kicked his horse forward, hitting the thing full force and trampling the creature until it was a broken pile. Its skinny arms and legs snapped like twigs from the impact.

The horse shuddered from the collision but seemed uninjured.

Looking back, Chip saw the teeth and clawed demon with the missing hand running at them again. This time, Chase slowed considerably, allowing it to reach him first. Right before it did, he wrapped the reigns around the little girl before him and spun around completely. As the demon lunged, he swung his sword in a wide two-handed arc, severing its head, which flew off in a different direction from the creature's body. Spinning back, he unwound the reigns from Beth and rejoined them. It was over in moments. Chip shook his head in wonder as Chase flashed him his notorious grin.

The pursuit ended as the remaining demons, not built for speed, fell behind the galloping horses.

The companions reached the first of the three towns and rode through its vacant streets without slowing. A short while later, the second town came into view, and they eased the horses to a canter to give them a chance to rest. It felt eerie going through the deserted villages. Usually, the towns would be bustling with activity at this time of day. Instead, nothing moved, and the air felt heavy with impending doom. A sinister silence accompanied them down the vacant streets.

As they rode, the wind picked up, and the sky darkened further to the west. The sun had almost disappeared, and the world took on a grey pall. Chip knew the storm could only mean one thing: The demon army was nearing the gates, and Elohan was bringing his Power to bear.

As if in answer, a jagged streak of lightning illuminated the dark clouds in the distance, sending a shiver down his spine. The small boy before him put on a brave face and stared defiantly into the wind. His little sister, on Chase's horse, looked frightened as her eyes darted left then right.

Chip put a hand on the child's shoulder. "You will be safe soon," he whispered in the boy's ear. He hoped it was true.

Han turned and smiled. "I believe in you."

The little boy's comment surprised Chip, revealing a sad emptiness the orphan had carried his whole life. No one had ever said that to him before. That a small, innocent child would put faith in the orphan gave him validation that he was worth something. It filled Chip with a sense of purpose and rightness. He would not let Han down.

They continued moving through the second town, but something did not seem right. Several front doors lining the streets were wide open like gaping, empty eye sockets. He did not remember them being open before. Soft, distant mewling sounds confirmed his suspicions. The demons were already here.

A chord of cold fear ran through him as he realized the demon army might reach the gates before them. They would be trapped and hopelessly surrounded. The boys had underestimated how quickly the horde could move. This was not a regular army that walked or marched. It was a ravenous full-fledged swarm of creatures intent on killing and devouring.

He looked at the dark, empty doors on either side. They seemed like portals of death in the deepening gloom. The mewling sounds were getting louder. There was a bend in the road ahead, and as soon as they rounded it, Chip glanced behind one more time to ensure there was no pursuit. As he did, something large and grey charged out of a roadside bush where the street turned. He did not see it coming.

The creature had four springy legs, a lion's head, and immense jaws full of razor-sharp teeth. As he turned back, the demon sailed through the air with its mouth opened wide. He knew he could not react in time and tried to raise his hands as the jaws closed to cleave him in two.

At that moment, something even larger leapt over his horse from the opposite side, slamming into the lion demon as it started closing its monstrous jaws. A howl of pain erupted from the creature as both beasts tumbled off the road. Chip had time to note silver and grey fur before realizing it was a huge mountain wolf.

After a brief flurry of activity, the wolf stood over the lion demon, who lay dead below it, throat torn open. The immense dog let out a mournful howl. It had the same silver fur running down its back as the one in the forest. He could not believe how big it was. Could it be the same one?

Chip galloped away, letting out a silent prayer to the Creator for his luck.

One last village was ahead before the final sprint to the gates. This was the one where Chase had fought the men in the tavern, telling the barkeep and his family to leave immediately. The wind picked up as the sounds of thunder began reverberating throughout the valley.

They entered the town warily. Both boys rode with swords in

hand, and Farn grimly gripped his axe. They reached the tavern without seeing any signs of demons in the growing darkness. It was deathly quiet. Chip knew he could not pass through without checking if the barkeep's family had made it out. The boy pulled up on the reins and leapt nimbly off his horse. He grabbed Han and passed him to his mother, Sally. Chase did the same with Beth.

"Stay here," Chase ordered Farn as he passed her off. "We will only be a moment."

The boys pushed open the tavern door and slipped inside. It took a moment for their eyes to adjust in the gloom. When they did, the sight of several half-eaten bodies greeted them, along with a gagging stench. What drew their eyes the most was the huge demon crouched in the middle of the room, feeding on the pot-bellied man beneath it.

A dying fire in the hearth gave illumination to the terrifying multi-legged creature. Its back was to them, but as soon as they entered, the demon spun around, placing its front forelegs on the half-eaten stomach of its victim. It had six other legs protruding from a round, hairy body almost identical to a giant spider.

The most terrifying feature was its demonic face, which contained black almond eyes filled with evil menace. Upon seeing the elven blade, it hissed and revealed sharp incisors protruding from a vertical mouth.

"I hate spiders," muttered Chase. As if in response, the spider demon skittered across the floor, crashing into them with incredible speed. They both held their swords straight out as the only mechanism of defence. The monstrous body impaled itself upon both blades, but its weight slammed them backwards. Chase grunted and flew out the open front door, tumbling end over end while Chip slammed into the wall. He felt the wind fly out of him but refused to fall.

The creature stumbled back in pain from the sword thrusts to its torso, which oozed thick, black demon blood. This only served to enrage it further, and it ran straight at the orphan. Chip was able to dive sideways and avoid most of the impact. The boy swung the elven blade down as he landed on his side. It sliced through one of the thing's legs, sending black blood spurting out of the severed appendage.

The spider demon spun around, hissing violently, and slammed its forelegs against Chip's chest. Out of reflex, he saw the Wall in his mind and was about to reach for his Power when Chase reappeared to leap on the monster's back, stabbing down through its triangular head. The tip of his friend's sword came out of its open mouth, nearly skewering Chip. The spider-like creature spasmed and flew upwards, almost crushing Chase against the ceiling. Chip was able to roll away before the body landed with a heavy thud exactly where he had been. It gave one last shudder and stopped moving. His best friend removed his sword and leapt off its hairy back, landing on his feet.

"Hard to train for that one," Chase said with relief.

Chip nodded in agreement. "I thought I was going to get squished for sure." He climbed gingerly to his feet. "Let's check the barkeep's family."

They looked into the back kitchen area, but there was no sign of the owner or his family. The boys returned to the main room to examine what looked like three corpses. Half-eaten body parts lay strewn around the room. The pot-bellied man and his two friends had paid the ultimate price for not heeding their warnings.

A sudden shout from outside made them run for the door. The pair burst from the tavern to see Farn pointing down the street in the direction they had come. A horde of demons at the far edge of town were running their way. He signalled to Chase, and they placed the children back on the horses, then leapt up behind them. Spurring their mounts forward at a full gallop, they left the town behind and rode into a darkening landscape. Squeals sounded behind them as the demons gave chase. Dark clouds were now directly overhead, and a strong wind blew in from the west. The countryside whipped by in a blur.

In the distance, the city appeared before them, a bastion of light and warmth. An encroaching darkness surrounded Vanalon in all directions, creating a shrinking oasis of light. Looking up, they noticed the sky blackening, yet it was not even midday. The demon horde behind them grew larger. Sounds began to reach the small party from the sides, and dark shapes appeared in the trees.

Chip realized that individual demons were running into the valley from all directions. These were faster than the main force but served the purpose of emptying the valley of life. These creatures were thorough in their singular goal of destroying everything in their path.

Urging the labouring horses harder, they could see Vanalon's gates getting closer. Then, from the road where the western wall curved, the front ranks of the demon army appeared. In their lead was a cloaked figure riding a monstrous black creature surrounded by a dozen others jogging alongside. They seemed more human than demonic.

For a terrifying moment, Chip thought it was the Unnamed One surrounded by his Inner Circle. Then, the lead figure threw off his hood and revealed himself as Elohan. He was riding what appeared to be an enormous reptilian creature covered in shiny scales. The terrifying beast had large black wings folded to its sides. Chip knew that dragons existed in the stories of old, yet they were supposed to be extinct. The beasts of legend had fought for the elves after the Breaking. None had survived, at least according to the stories.

The figures running beside Elohan looked to be Dark Elves. Chip risked another glance behind and, with chagrin, saw that the demon horde from the town was closing in fast. Despite that, it still looked like they had enough time to reach the gates. To the other side of them, the main army was rounding the final bend in the road leading into the city. They had made it down from the valley rim shockingly fast. The companions pushed their horses to the limits, making a final dash for the gates. They were only a few hundred feet away.

Elohan, sitting atop the black dragon, noticed what they were attempting and grinned wickedly. His half-melted face looked more evil than ever. Raising his arms, the Dark Elf clapped his hands, and ear-splitting thunder echoed above. Then, bringing his hands straight down, an arc of lightning appeared from on high and came hurtling towards them. Chip had no choice and instinctively reached for the Wall in his mind.

"Don't." Xander's voice echoed in his head.

The boy paused as a long arc of blue flame shot from the top of the city walls to form a bright shield above their heads. Elohan's deadly lightning disappeared into the blue barrier. Both lights then disappeared. The wizard had protected them.

The small party spurred their horses onward with newfound energy, racing for the gates. They reached the main road directly in front of the approaching army. The demons behind them shrieked maniacally, closing in. The gates were open enough to let them through if they could make it in time. The demon force was now on the final stretch, moving fast. Chip looked behind them, and his blood ran cold.

The creature under Elohan opened its massive wings and leapt into the air. The sound of its beating wings was palpable. The Dark Inner Circle Elf sat atop the black dragon, holding its reins, smiling menacingly. His dark brown cloak stayed still despite the unnatural wind.

An intense beam of blue light suddenly erupted from the top of the gates, slamming into the dragon's chest. The air crackled with energy. The monstrosity recoiled briefly as it absorbed the magic, apparently unharmed. Suspended in mid-air in front of the gates of Vanalon, the black dragon opened its enormous mouth full of razor-sharp teeth and took a huge breath.

Dark energy filled its chest from within, and Chip watched in awe as a huge black flame exploded from its jaws, blasting towards the gates. The fire streaked over their heads, straight at the soldiers standing on top of the wall, incinerating them. The gates ignited in an inferno of flame. The force and heat of the fire overhead caused the horses of the two boys to crash into each other. They both went down in a tangled heap.

Chip did his best to throw Han clear as he tumbled and rolled. Chase threw Beth to safety as he fell but was having difficulty extricating himself from his horse. Farn and Sally kept their mount upright as they pulled on the reins to stop. The two small children ran for each other and hugged.

Before Chip could respond, Elohan flicked his wrist casually. The black dragon swooped down with its massive jaws and snapped them shut on Farn and his wife Sally, killing them instantly. The old horse's back broke from the force, and it slumped to the ground. With both bodies dangling from its mouth, the dragon viciously threw them sideways into the demon horde, which tore the lifeless humans apart.

Chip screamed in horror.

Beth and Han were all alone in the middle of the road, clinging tightly to each other. The orphan stood behind the children in disbelief. The dragon's wings seemed to beat in slow motion as it hung suspended in the air above them. Elohan, sitting on the back of the beast, saw Chip's expression and smiled fully, revealing sharp white teeth. The Dark Elf looked down at the two tiny children before him. Beth cried uncontrollably into Han's chest while the little boy looked up. His face held defiance. Surrounded on three sides by a demon army full of terrifying creatures, the small boy stared unflinchingly at the black dragon. The gates of Vanalon burned brightly behind them. Chip saw Han holding his tiny sister amidst a sea of horror and knew why humanity must survive.

5

Elohan leaned forward to smile at the children, then let out a cold laugh and whispered to his dragon, pointing at them. Its fangs dripped blood as the beast peered at the two little beings in front of it. The rest of the demon army stopped to watch expectantly. Farn's broken horse lay at the creature's feet.

The black dragon breathed in deep, its chest filling up. Elohan wanted to incinerate them. His laugh turned into a sickening cackle. The rest of the demons began shrieking in anticipation.

A rage filled Chip like nothing he had ever experienced in his life.

He strode forward to stand in front of the children. The wizard's warning not to use his Power meant nothing to him anymore. He had no choice but to fight this monstrous evil. Moreover, he wanted to.

The boy shattered the Wall to his Power as if it did not exist. His eyes exploded with blazing red energy. Elohan's high laugh cut short, replaced by shock, then fear.

Chip felt fury like no other.

He pulled the Power into himself like a tidal wave. The Dark Elf jerked frantically at the reigns of the dragon as it tried to incinerate them. It was too late. Chip's hands flew out, releasing a torrent of red fire that smote the dragon directly in the chest.

Elohan flew off its back like a rag doll, cartwheeling off into the horde. The impact melted the dragon's scales as if they were paper. Chip filled the creature to bursting with a massive stream of red-hot fire, then opened his hands. The black dragon held for a moment and then simply exploded, pieces of its body flying in all directions.

Chase, free of his horse, ran forward and scooped up Han and Beth. The demons paused at the spectacle. Only the Unnamed One had red eyes, so they seemed unsure of what was happening. The Dark Elves in front of the horde screamed and pointed at him. The demons hesitated for another moment, then surged forward as one.

Chip could see two Dark Elves carrying Elohan's body off the field. He was not moving. The boy's rage sprang anew, and as the demons closed in on all sides, he lifted his hands and swept them in a deadly arc. Red fire flew from his fingers into the demon's front lines, completely vaporizing them. The Dark Elves in the middle formed a shield of magic with their combined Power, but it could not withstand the red fire. The ones in front began to fall and melt.

"Get back!" he heard someone scream behind him. Chip turned and, through a red haze, saw Chase calling to him. For a moment, he was about to walk back into the demon horde to continue dealing death and destruction, but somewhere in his mind, he realized there were too many. The boy backed up with his best friend, sending streaks of red fire at any demons who came close. The creatures were having trouble climbing over the melted remains of the ones in front. Others were half-burnt and writhing on the ground, causing further chaos. For a moment, they were in the clear.

"Put the Wall back up," Xander ordered, appearing next to him. His robes were singed, likely from the dragon fire. Chip nodded with some effort and finally released the Power. He wanted to leave his Wall down but followed the wizard's instructions. A sudden weariness engulfed him, and he stumbled.

They pulled him back through the smouldering gates, which clanged shut. Several soldiers ran up to reinforce the huge doors by bracing wood and other objects against the half-melted metal.

The orphan felt tired but brushed it aside as he searched for Han and Beth. He found them at the side of the gates, being consoled by Princess Eleanor. Han's face lit up when he saw Chip. Beth's crying paused for a moment as he hugged them both. Xander and Chase stood to the side.

"I'm sorry I couldn't save your parents," Chip said, fighting back tears. Han nodded sadly. He tried to put on a brave face.

"You killed the bad dragon," the little boy said and hugged Chip again. Then he turned once more to console his sister.

"Please get them to safety. They must leave the city." The boy looked at Eleanor, who nodded with tears in her eyes. The princess was staring at him with a strange look.

"It's not your fault," the wizard said. "The dragon was unexpected."

Chip wheeled on him, his face furious. "I could have stopped the dragon before it killed them. You told me not to use my Power!" He had never yelled at the wizard before. He was suddenly aware that everyone was looking at him. Chip realized that none of them, other than the weapons master and the wizard, knew about his Power until now. Chase, for once, was speechless, a mixture of emotions playing across his face.

Xander gave the boy a stern but compassionate look. "The human mind is a powerful weapon, but it can sabotage itself by laying blame. Not revealing your Power was the most prudent course at the time, but when the dragon proved too strong, we had to change strategies. Do not burden yourself with what-if scenarios or guilt. Blaming others will make you a victim and powerless or, worse, powerful in the wrong way. Forgive readily and understand we are all human, Chip. We will all make choices that might look like mistakes in the coming days. If they are, then we learn from them and move on. I do not pretend to know the Creator's will or if the Creator really exists. I do know that those two children are alive because of you." His face turned serious. "We still have a demon army at the gates." The wizard looked around. "Back to your posts."

Chip felt a hand on his shoulder. It was Garth Stone. "Your bravery is why those children are alive and a dragon is dead. The stories of old say there were many types of dragons, but the fire-breathing ones were by far the strongest. Not even Xander's magic could have saved us from that beast. You did well. Remember, a wise person blames no one."

He squeezed the boy's shoulder and ran up the stairs to the top of the wall. Chip followed to see what was happening. When they reached the top, he stood beside the commander and looked down upon the demon army.

The creatures had pulled back to remove the bodies of their brethren and pieces of the dragon. The Dark Elves left alive were in a circle conferring. Chase appeared on his other side, still looking at him in wonder. Chip tried to smile but felt another wave of weariness.

Garth looked sideways at him. "Using the Power takes a toll on all magic wielders. Using that much Power…" He shook his head. "I am surprised you are still standing. I have never seen such a thing."

"How did that dragon survive?" Chip asked. The weapons master shook his head.

"I do not know, and neither does Xander. They supposedly died out centuries before the Great Battle. The Light and Dark Elves pitted them against each other during the Elf Wars until none remained. Most were not fire-breathing. They were ferocious beasts, but only a few had that singular Power, which manifested as black or white fire, depending on their colour. They are intelligent and fiercely loyal. Their fire is unique to them. They are essentially breathing magic at you. Your magic was stronger than even the black dragons. It could not withstand your Power, which is quite remarkable. Perhaps we have a chance to win this war after all, albeit small." He allowed a rare smile, making Chip feel better. Noticing the mood change, Garth leaned in. "We must steel our hearts in war. Before this is over, we will see more death than you can imagine. All of us may perish in the end. However, we gave an oath to defend Vanalon and the human race. Let's fulfill that oath."

He turned back to the army before the city.

The demons had formed a solid line. Chip looked at the smoking gates and wondered how long they would hold. He saw Princess Eleanor escorting Han and Beth away from the walls. A woman was waiting for them at the edge of the square. With relief, he saw it was Auntie Clare. She must have been summoned to take the children to safety. Eleanor turned back and pointed up at him. The children and Auntie Clare all waved. He felt strong emotions and waved back. The head midwife ushered the children ahead of her. They were going to Calgar and could not be in better hands. Chase moved to stand beside him and looked at the orphan appraisingly.

"A wizard, eh? You could have told me." He looked away, staring at his nails.

"Xander forbade me to tell anyone, even you. Trust me, I wanted to." He looked down.

Chase slapped him on the shoulder. "It's alright. If you didn't use that magic, we would be charcoal right now." He laughed. "My best friend is a wizard!" Chip looked relieved. Chase turned back to the demons, serious once again. "Now I want my vengeance against those monsters for what they did to Farn and Sally."

Chip nodded wholeheartedly as he watched Xander climb nimbly up the stairs to stand with the two boys. The dark clouds were leaving, revealing the sun and the wind had died. Without Elohan's Power sustaining it, the weather was returning to normal. It was a sunny autumn day.

The wizard squinted at the horde. "Despite being unnatural monsters, the demons are disciplined. In the accompaniment of Dark Elves, the creatures follow all orders without question. They rarely feel fear. Left on their own, they only seek to kill and feed, but with their masters, they form a powerful army. With the black dragon, they would have easily been victorious today. My blue fire was not able to seriously harm such an enemy. Its black fire would have laid waste to the city and destroyed us all.

"The Demon King has received two hard blows today. His black dragon is dead, and one of his Inner Circle, Elohan, has failed him. The Dark Elves might be able to heal him, but he may wish otherwise. The Unnamed One does not suffer failure lightly. Even so, our brief victory has cost us much. The Demon King now knows who you are. He has read the prophecy in the Ancient City. His sole goal beyond conquering this world will be to kill you. His knowledge of the histories is vast. Despite his evil, he knows there is a Balance and that whatever forces that be have put you in his path. Only one of you can survive. He will strike while you are still young and inexperienced. Besides, you killed his dragon."

He looked at the boy with an air of sympathy.

Despite the gravity of the situation, Chip could not help but grin. "True, but you stole his Orb of Power." The wizard tried to maintain a serious face but could not.

"True as well. It looks like we are at the top of his list of enemies." The old man sighed. "We are still in grave danger. For now, we must repel this demon advance."

Even as he spoke, the front lines began marching towards the wall. A cold chill rippled through the men. Chip was amazed by the incredible variations in demon size and form as they drew closer. Some were small and nimble, while others had large bear-like bodies built for strength and power. There were tall, skinny runners for speed and spider-like ones of all sizes. Several looked like fearsome pigs with large tusks, while others had long, stick-like arms ending in points for jabbing. Interspersed throughout were the teeth and claws type he had fought on the bridge. They were quick and dangerous. He looked along the wall and saw the soldiers defending the city go pale with fear. The weapons master also noticed the men's reaction.

"They bleed like all creatures," Garth Stone shouted to them. "Use your fear as energy. Remember your training. Above all, remember your oath. We do not fight for ourselves. We fight for all humankind." The high commander raised his sword. The men cheered and followed suit.

In response, the ranks opened in the middle of the demons, and a well-hidden battering ram emerged from the center of the horde. Eight demons with heavily muscled legs pushed the crossbeams of the enormous cart the ram rested on and rushed forward. The gates were buttressed by all manner of equipment and heavy objects, but it would not hold long against such force.

"Let me burn it with my magic," Chip whispered to Xander.

"No," the wizard said, "nobody knows the limits of your magic, not even you. You expended a tremendous amount of Power killing the dragon. I saw you sway from your efforts. Save your energy until there is no choice. I also do not want you to become their target." He calmly stepped in front of the boy. "Besides, it's my turn."

Xander pointed both hands at the massive battering ram, which had almost reached the gates. Two streaks of blue fire burst forth from his fingers and struck the immense log. It exploded into flames, burning all the demons pushing it forward. Fiery sparks flew into the horde. They screamed and released the crossbeams. The fire engulfed the whole ram, setting it ablaze.

In response, a ball of green roiling fire flew from the center of the Dark Elves towards the wizard. Xander turned and moved his hands in a circular motion, forming a blue shield that absorbed the fire. The Dark Elves shouted angrily, and the one in front lifted a horn to blow a long, low note. On cue, the entire demon army charged the walls.

"Archers!" the weapons master commanded. "Release at will!"

Fifty men on top of the wall fitted and released arrows at the running demons, impaling scores of the shrieking creatures. Screams filled the air. The soldiers continued to fire volley after volley.

The frenzied demons ran forward with hate and rage, some with several arrows in them like pincushions. As they neared the walls, great swaths of ground collapsed into huge holes the men had dug when fortifying the city. The demons piled in, impaling themselves on the sharpened spears below. The traps worked to perfection. Many of the foul creatures, mindlessly following the ones in front, fell into the holes after them. The clever ones who sidestepped the pits fell through other trap doors farther on and suffered the same fate. The losses were huge, and finally, the Dark Elf blew the horn again, this time signalling retreat.

The demons pulled back, gnashing their teeth in frustration. Many were too injured to retreat and lay where they were, whimpering in agony. Others struggled but could not remove the spears that impaled them. Some tried to claw their way out of the pits but could not escape the weight of those lying on top. When they could finally wriggle free, the archers picked them off.

Demons lay dead all along the front wall. The trenches and pits had been cleverly hidden with flat cloth tied across them, then covered with dirt and grass.

Half the demon army was now injured or dead. The traps had done their job. The men clapped each other on the back. They had not suffered a single loss. Chip looked over at the weapons master, but he did not celebrate. Instead, he was staring intently at the horde.

Chip followed the high commander's gaze in time to see a shadowy figure step forward from behind the Dark Elves. He wore a cloak of midnight black. Xander turned, and his face went white.

"Morgo," he gasped. He looked at Chip in fear. "Run!"

Garth and Xander were suddenly lifted into the air by an unseen hand. The wizard's eyes blazed bright blue, but it was too late. Both of them flew backwards off the wall. Chip screamed as he watched them fall. Chase tried to seize the wizard's cloak, but it slipped through his fingers.

The pair fell as if in slow motion, then crashed into the furniture piled before the gate. Dust and debris flew in the air. Garth seemed stunned but started moving almost immediately. The wizard lay deathly still.

The orphan's rage ignited, and he reached for his Wall, but something was wrong. A powerful presence barred his way. The boy pushed with all his might.

"Still very strong despite your efforts today, impressive." The voice in his mind was like a silky hiss. "I am Morgo, general of all demons, second to the Unnamed One, may we grovel at his leisure."

Chip looked back over the wall at the demon horde. Morgo was walking alone down the road approaching the gates. The archers on the walls had seen what happened to their commander and were firing furiously at the figure. The arrows hit his black cloak and fell harmlessly to the ground. He seemed to crackle with dark energy.

Chip looked down and saw the weapons master dragging the limp wizard to the side. Queen Charlotte ran up to Xander's inert form. Eleanor joined them, her face etched in concern. She looked up at Chip, and their eyes met.

Without warning, the boy levitated into the air. The princess screamed. Chase stood by helplessly. An unseen force spun Chip around to face Morgo, who was almost at the gates. The boy desperately fought to reach the Wall and access his Power, but the presence in his mind was immovable.

"My Master will want to torment you personally for killing his black dragon, Fang. You will suffer more pain than any living creature to the end of your days." Chip went cold with fear.

Morgo stood in front of the gates and casually pointed one gloved hand. An immense crackling ball of black energy shot from his fingers, exploding into the giant doors and ripping them off their hinges. They flew backwards into several buildings, completely collapsing them. A soldier who had been standing in front of one of the buildings died instantly. Screams erupted everywhere. Several men rushed at Morgo through the gaping hole with swords swinging.

Using his other hand, the general picked them up as one and slammed them with ferocious Power into the side of the wall. They crumpled, broken and lifeless. Chip hung helplessly in the air. His fear was overwhelming. The boy frantically sought the Calm, which was as elusive as ever. He forced himself to focus on the dead soldiers lying in a heap. A spark of raw anger ignited, reducing his fear enough to locate the Calm. Then, a voice entered his head.

"Morgo is tricking you..." It was Xander! Chip looked around and spotted the wizard propped up by Queen Charlotte off to the side. They were looking up at the boy with concern. Hope surged through him, and he surrounded himself in the Calm.

"Xandrostika cannot help you, boy," Morgo hissed with an edge of irritation. "He will be made an example of for all eternity. His meddling imprisoned us for three millennia."

An unimaginable hatred infused his voice. Chip focused on the presence blocking his Wall. For a moment, the Wall revealed itself as

Morgo's anger let slip a slight crack. It looked different. Something was wrong. As if reading Chip's thoughts, Morgo reasserted his presence. The Wall disappeared, out of reach. Chip decided to remain in the Calm. He observed his own mind. Something was out of place, but he could not figure out what.

"I will now allow the people to see my true form and know fear."

Morgo strode into the city past the gates. Arrows rained down on him with no effect. The general removed his black hood. The sight made the men gasp. He had a reptilian face covered in intricate tattooed symbols. The patterns intertwined and seemed to interact with and move on their own. He was not human or elf anymore. The only similarity between him and the Dark Elves was his black eyes. A strange dark magic surrounded him, seeming to dampen and drain the energy of life itself. The light in his vicinity became muted and wan. If ever there was a creature of evil and death, this was it.

The soldiers shrank backwards at the sight, and a helpless fear chilled their hearts. Some broke down and started crying, bereft of hope. A few dropped their weapons. Chip felt the Calm warble, and he clutched for a positive thought. For a moment, he felt hopeless and decided it might be best to surrender without a fight.

Yet as the thought entered his mind, he felt every core of his being fight it. He knew once, long ago, what it was like to give up and surrender. Back then, he had consciously decided to live and looked Death itself in the eye, staying its hand. This creature was not Death. Instead, he sensed it somehow used death and darkness as a means to trade for life energy. It had found a way to drain life to sustain its consciousness. Death had allowed such a dark pact.

In the serenity of the Calm, Chip could see through this creature's subterfuge. It robbed men of hope and thought. It used dark magic propagated by dark arts and spells to harness the life energy of those around it. Unlike the Power, which could be used for good or evil, this creature siphoned the energy of life to sustain its dark energy. Chip realized the inscribed symbols on its face and body were somehow crafted to trade the life energy around it with the dark energy of

Death. It used trickery and illusion to take away the will to fight. The truth of this creature struck Chip in the Calm.

Despite this knowledge, he knew Morgo was more dangerous than any being he had ever met. The general had fed on the energy of life and others' Powers for a long time. He knew Morgo was the one who taught the Demon King how to drink the white-eyed demons' Power. He needed to learn more. Instinctively, he surrounded Morgo with the Calm in his mind, as he did to Elohan on the bridge. The creature, so sure of itself, was unaware he slipped into its consciousness. Memories flooded him, and he was thrust into Morgo's world. Chip searched for the general's origins.

Images of a small village surrounded by swamp enveloped the orphan. Morgo's first memory showed all the villagers staring up at the sky, which was lit by a multitude of colours, including red. Great waves of light and fire swirled through the heavens. The people were witnessing a great magic of unknown origin. Chip's mind reeled. The boy realized that Morgo had seen the Great Forget five millennia ago! This creature was older than everyone. Though the cause might remain unknown, the Great Forget was indeed a magical event with immense ripple effects.

As the villagers watched the Great Forget, they forgot what happened before and where they came from. A flurry of memories rushed by. Chip could piece together that the villagers were hard-working fishermen who also hunted a rare breed of giant snake. The venom, if used in minute quantities, cured a variety of ailments. People came from far and wide to heal their conditions.

A young fisherman named Ben stared intently at the lights, and suddenly, the pupils of his eyes turned black as night. He was struck with jealousy, envy, and paranoia. He believed the other villagers wanted the great snakes he caught for themselves. They looked greedily at his possessions, even though they never tried to take them, but he knew they wanted to. Whenever they whispered, he knew they were talking about him. When they thought he was not looking, he would whip around and catch them staring at him. Finally, he could not take it anymore and began to murder them secretly. The other villagers accused each other of the murders, but he could tell by their whispers that they thought it was him.

One day, his neighbour Kem caught him in the act of killing one of the villagers. Kem attacked Ben, who tried to fight back, but his neighbour was much larger and overpowered him. Kem struck him repeatedly in the face and body until Ben felt something snap in his mind. He saw a Wall and broke through it. The young fisherman then found a small Power and used it to knock his attacker to the ground. It dazed the neighbour, and Ben was able to grab a fishing spear off the wall and impale him. A weak yellow light shone from his eyes when he used his Power. He felt a thrill of invincibility course through him. The Power in his mind was like a drug, and he sought more of it. However, he only had a tiny amount.

The other villagers could not prove he was the murderer in the village but now strongly suspected him once they found his dead neighbour. They banded together and drove him out. As they did, the villagers changed his name from Ben to Morgo, which meant "Murderer" in their dialect.

Images flashed of Morgo wandering different lands to find knowledge of the Power. Libraries contained no books on history. All the records started with an event called the Great Magic and continued from there. Nobody could remember what happened before that. They eventually called it the Great Forget.

The general's sole desire was to increase his Power. It was the driving force of his life. After banishment from the village, he spent many years searching different cities in faraway lands. He strove to attain more Power, for his was woefully small. Morgo found a way to permanently remove the Wall to his Power so he would never be without its soothing touch. When he used up his little Power too greedily, the man suffered a deep, horrible yearning until it replenished. He was drawn to books on witchcraft and dark magic. Most were fraudulent or full of impotent spells.

Morgo began to lose hope until one day he heard about a "Magic Man" spoken of by superstitious villagers on the outskirts of Amrika. The man lived in a cave like a hermit deep in the northern mountains in the east of the Troll Kingdom. Venturing this far from civilization was dangerous, but he did not care. Even the faintest possibility of a method to harness more Power motivated Morgo to risk everything.

After a journey fraught with perils and pitfalls, he finally found the magic man deep in the mountains. The hermit offered him a bargain. The Magic Man would show him how to draw on another's Power, and in exchange, Morgo had to give the man his humanity, which was what the hermit desired above all else. The Magic Man confided that he was not human and needed these gifts to stay transformed as a man.

Morgo agreed to the bargain, and upon release of his humanity, the general's features altered to those of a snake. It was the creature he identified with the most. In exchange, the Magic Man drew intricate spell symbols on Morgo's face, allowing him to sense another's magic at great distances, even when they were not using it, provided they had reached an age when they had already broken through their Walls. The primary purpose of the symbols was to allow him to siphon off Power from another magic wielder, provided they granted him access.

Upon completing the exchange, Morgo looked in a pool of water, revealing a mirror image of his reptilian face. He screamed in horror, realizing he would never be accepted anywhere with that countenance.

The hermit then offered him another bargain. The Magic Man would give him the Power to shape-shift and conceal his new image. Morgo told him he would do anything to gain this skill, so in return, the hermit asked for his spirit essence or soul. If given, Morgo would essentially be dead, but Death itself would animate him by allowing access to its dark energy. This energy would forever drain the life out of his surroundings, which would serve to sustain him. Also, by relinquishing his spirit essence, he would not feel pain. His magic would be black. He alone would command such a dark energy and use it to alter his appearance to any being he had taken the life of. It would also make him extremely difficult to kill. Morgo would furthermore be long-lived like no other.

The general agreed to the bargain, and the exchange was made. His strength grew from his access to the power of Death, but it was still limited by the space his spirit essence occupied. Death allowed him a perpetual but finite amount of its dark energy in exchange for the many souls he would send its way over the millennia.

Yet Morgo sought more Power still.

As he left the hermit's cave, a rogue troll party ran across him in the frozen wasteland of the north. Morgo was only wearing a black cloak, as cold did not affect him anymore. The huge mountain trolls, covered in thick animal fur and wielding heavy clubs, surrounded his hooded form.

The general reached into his newfound dark Power and shot black death at them from splayed fingers. They fell before him like straw. The use of his new Power electrified him, but it was still finite. He was ten times stronger than before, but the space it contained in his mind remained the same. He spent the next few centuries seeking people with Power and feeding off them after they granted the dead man access. Only when he revealed his natural reptilian face and the spells etched on his skin could he draw on their Power, if they were a willing host.

Morgo would teach his donors aspects of the Dark Arts in trade for their Power, becoming a formidable ally. He leached Power from many great men and women over the ages, controlling these people and influencing powerful nations and history itself.

The memories leapt forward. Chip saw Morgo standing in a beautiful forest, watching a red-eyed young elven prince frolicking on a beautiful sunny day. The dead man was naturally drawn to the Power of this prince from far away. His name was Killian. Not much more than a boy, Prince Killian ran through the forest with wild abandon, laughing in pure joy at the sound and smells of nature.

Morgo had extreme sensitivity to Power and could feel it at great distances. Up close, he shook from the immense Power harboured in this young elven prince. He had never felt anything like it. Morgo had no interest in fame or recognition, only the desire for more Power. He always remained in the background. He never revealed his true form until he knew the host would grant him access to their Power. As he walked the Earth, Morgo could shape-shift into any dead being he chose, as long as they died by his own hand.

Chip watched as the dead man altered his form to that of a wise old elf hermit who lived on his own. He showed the young elf prince little magic tricks and things he could do with his Power. Memories flashed of Morgo cultivating a relationship with Killian, teaching him the Dark Arts. The general eventually showed the prince how to remove his Wall permanently. It was then that he revealed his true form. By then, Killian did not care and agreed to share some of his monstrous Power. Soon after, Prince Killian gathered followers and murdered his father, causing the Breaking. They became known as the Dark Elves.

Memories of Killian holding the Orb of Power surfaced. Chip saw the Demon King and Morgo rage when they realized the orb was missing. Then, he watched the demon army fleeing to a large island after the Great Battle. A disturbing memory briefly surfaced of Morgo offering a demon baby with white eyes for his Master to eat.

Chip's last image was of the Unnamed One standing on a towering rock at the end of Demon Island, facing the new, shining barrier. The Demon King's blazing red eyes almost burst forth from his helmeted head as his gloved hands clenched in anger. A black flowing cape billowed behind him, and the dark sky danced with thunder and lightning. His Inner Circle knelt around him, wailing at his rage. He screamed a terrible sound and sent an incredible blast of red-hot fire into the barrier from his gloved hands to no avail. Killian screamed again, causing the demon army behind him to shriek and writhe in anguish at their Master's discontent.

Then the images vanished as Morgo pulled his mind out of the Calm. Only moments had passed as Chip read and absorbed those memories.

"You will pay for that intrusion." General Morgo stood inside the gates of Vanalon, facing up at the boy with a mixture of surprise and rage. He squeezed one hand, and Chip felt his lungs constrict.

Hanging in midair, the boy could not move or breathe. His

control over the Calm was slipping. Chip lashed out at the presence in his mind and, for a moment, saw the Wall again, but Morgo quickly blocked it from view. This time, he realized it was not the real Wall. The general was tricking him. Unable to breathe, he calmly turned and found the real Wall in his mind, which materialized from his recognition of the illusion. Chip realized it had been there all along. He reached for it, but his vision went black from lack of air.

Suddenly, the grip released him. Chip sucked in fresh air and landed on his feet atop the city wall. He struggled to stay upright, riding a wave of dizziness. Looking down, the boy saw Xander shooting blue fire at the general across the courtyard. Morgo looked surprised that the wizard could still use magic. The general had released Chip to use both hands to shoot black fire back at the wizard.

The two fires met in midair, and Morgo's black magic inexorably pushed the blue fire back. Xander's bloody face contorted in dismay as the general overpowered him. Several soldiers sat on the ground holding their heads as Morgo's presence leeched all hope out of them.

Queen Charlotte stepped forward next to the wizard with fierce determination on her face. The small woman unleashed a thin stream of yellow fire, which joined the blue to fight the general. Many soldiers and civilians gasped in shock that their queen was a magic wielder. Sadly, it was not enough. Morgo pushed harder until the wizard and the queen screamed in pain as the black fire began to consume them.

Chip's head cleared.

He needed no more fuel for his rage. The boy blasted through the Wall in his mind and filled himself with Power until he shook. Morgo turned, sensing what was happening. The general released his stream of dark energy, and the wizard and queen collapsed in a smoking heap, exhausted. Pointing both hands, Morgo unleashed a torrent of black fire straight at the boy, his face a mask of hate.

"No." Chip raised his hands and sent his Power out to meet the general's black magic in a blinding red explosion. His magic split the dark energy. A thick line of red fire continued, striking the general square in the chest, sending him hurtling thirty feet backwards into the city wall. His black robes caught fire.

The boy filled himself with more Power and aimed both hands to finish him off. Quick as thought, the general slithered naked out of his burning robes, exposing his ghastly reptilian body. He had thick green, mottled skin with skinny arms and legs. His face did not register any pain from the impact of striking the wall, but dark blood oozed from his tail.

As he snaked forward, Morgo sent a stream of dark energy directly into the base of the city wall Chip was standing on. The orphan unleashed a red ball of magic simultaneously but missed the general, who skittered away through the gates on all fours with uncanny speed, scampering back to the horde.

Chip's footing gave way as he felt the wall crumble below his feet. He tried to use his magic to slow the speed of his descent, forming a cushion of air. It was only partially successful, and he landed hard atop the rubble. Grimacing, the boy rose amidst the dust and debris and promptly fell back down as a wave of exhaustion struck him. He knew he had used much Power in battling the dragon and Morgo.

In the back of his mind, the orphan could hear the weapons master admonishing him to get up, as he had done countless times in training. Chip pushed aside his pain and sought the serenity of the Calm. He put his Wall back up and gritted his teeth through the pain and weariness until the Calm reduced them to a dull throb.

Gritting his teeth, the boy stood up, knowing the battle was far from over.

6

"Barricade the entrance!" the high commander shouted, running forward with a knot of soldiers and picking up pieces of anything they could find. Chip looked outside the city to see the demon horde running forward in full attack mode towards the broken gates. Morgo sat far in the distance against a tree overlooking the battlefield, tended to by Dark Elves. On a positive note, the city wall that collapsed under the boy had filled half the hole where the gates once stood. The weapons master and others were throwing everything they could find into the remaining empty spot.

"Use wood!" Chip yelled. "Set it on fire. They hate fire!"

Garth turned and nodded, ordering his men to find wood. "Archers!" he bellowed to the men still on the wall. "Shoot at will!"

Volleys of arrows rained down, and the demons in front fell in droves, slowing the advance. Some larger creatures needed several arrows before they went down. Fifty men atop the walls continued firing while the rest mobilized behind the makeshift barricade. The demons were almost at the gates, but a pile of wood now blocked the hole.

"Drop the pitch!" ordered Garth. As he said it, the demons were already clambering over the pile. The weapons master pulled his sword out smoothly and skewered a long, skinny creature that leapt on him from the top of the barricade. Other demons climbed nimbly over the furniture and pieces of metal, then launched themselves at anyone they could find. Two soldiers ran over and dumped a barrel of pitch onto the pile. Others poured several more barrels from the top of the wall.

The demons were now crawling over the entire fortification. Chip watched in fascination as the pitch falling from above covered some creatures head to toe in black goo. He knew the substance, mined from the earth, was highly flammable.

"Stand back from the barricade!" a voice boomed with authority. The men jumped backwards, swords in hand. The blockade had become a living, moving mass of demons, wood, metal, and pitch. Xander, white hair in disarray, stood at the back of the courtyard in his singed robe, arms raised. The wizard's eyes blazed bright, and a stream of blue fire exploded towards the moving pile.

When it struck, the pitch ignited with a loud pop. An immense wave of fire rushed across the whole mound, consuming dozens of demons trying to get through. Screams filled the air, and wails of inhuman pain rang out. The few creatures that made it to the courtyard were surrounded by the waiting soldiers and hacked to pieces. The horde outside shrank backwards in fear, shielding their eyes from the flames. Archers continued sending volleys into them without pause. Cheers erupted from the men in the courtyard.

Chip ran across the square to help Queen Charlotte rise. Princess Eleanor was holding her mother's hands. The queen had burn marks on her face, and her beautiful dress looked wilted. She smiled wearily at the boy and accepted his help getting to her feet.

"Thank you," she said to him gratefully. "We would have fallen without you. Morgo is incredibly powerful."

"Are you alright?" Eleanor asked Chip, and before he could respond, she hugged him tightly.

"I'm fine, I think," Chip managed. She finally let go as Xander walked up to him with a look of wonder.

"You managed to injure Morgo, a creature nearly unmatched in

Power. If you had not assisted us, I am afraid that would have been the end of our tale." He gripped the boy's shoulder in thanks, and then his face turned serious. "We still have an army to fight. The demons have suffered huge casualties, but a large force remains, ready to enter the city when the fire dies. One-on-one, we do not stand a chance. Our Powers are almost exhausted."

"I can help with that," an older woman chirped behind them. They turned to see Miss Owl, the schoolteacher, standing wearing a grey sweater to ward off the chill. Her eyes blazed a bright yellow behind her traditional thick spectacles. Chip's mouth dropped open.

"You are a wizard!"

"As a matter of fact, they used to call us sorceresses, but in these modern times, all male and female magic wielders are now wizards." She grabbed his hands, and a jolt of energy rushed into him before the boy could pull them back. He felt some of his exhaustion leave him. She let go a little wobbly, then grabbed Xander and did the same. When she released him, Miss Owl began falling sideways, but Chase propped her up with one hand, trying not to laugh.

"Perhaps that was a bit much," she said giddily. I think I'm going to go lie down." She held on to Chase's arm for a moment more before walking stiffly away from them until she disappeared around a corner.

"Thanks!" Chip called after her, but she was already gone. Queen Charlotte smiled. Eleanor turned to her.

"You knew, didn't you?" she said, looking at her mother with narrow eyes.

The queen nodded mischievously. "Miss Owl is a Yellow with exceptional healing skills. We trained at the Wizard's Guild together."

They heard several soldiers cry out atop the wall, pointing. Green energy surrounded the fiery mound blocking the gate, subduing the flames. They all raced across the courtyard to the other side and climbed the steps to stand on the still intact wall. Out of bowshot, the Dark Elves stood together with arms raised, directing their magic as one at the fire. They might be relatively weak individually, but together, they could raise considerable Power.

"Do we try and burn them?" Chip asked, raising his arms.

"No," Xander answered. "Miss Owl restored some of our Power, but it will exhaust quickly. Save it until necessary. Besides, they are too far away." He gestured to the weapons master. "Have the men find more furniture and wood to pile on the fire. Stack extra pitch to the side." Garth nodded and issued orders.

The Dark Elves extinguished the fire, and the remaining horde moved forward. The demons let out excited mewls as they ran ahead, but those sounds became shrieks of rage as new pitch-soaked firewood flared anew. In the meantime, the archers continued to fire into the horde, which had no choice but to retreat again. There was no sign of General Morgo.

The Dark Elves stepped well back to confer in a circle, then turned and issued orders to the demon army. Within moments, the creatures began a full retreat. Some men started cheering, but the commander held up his hand, indicating it was not over. They watched as the horde scurried back across the farmer's fields and disappeared into the forest.

The weapons master surveyed his soldiers. At this point, there were only a few casualties, as they were able to repel the assault.

Taking advantage of the lull, the commander barked orders. "Stay alert, men. You have defended the city honourably, but this battle is far from over. Restock your arrows and refill the pitch barrels. Every other man, take time to eat and rest, and then relieve your comrade. Stay close to the wall. If the horn sounds, get back to your post. The soldiers saluted and proceeded to carry out his commands. All of them showed complete respect for the weapons master.

The men atop the walls eyed the distant forest warily. Dead demons littered the entire field in front of the city. Many had fallen into the traps and impaled themselves. The continuous volley of arrows had felled countless more. Chip wondered what had happened to General Morgo.

The wizard turned to him as if reading his thoughts. "What did you see in his mind?" he inquired. "I tried to warn you of his tricks, but he pushed me out."

"I saw his memories," Chip answered, trembling. "He traded everything to satisfy his need for more Power. There is a "Magic Man" in the mountains near the troll kingdom that made him a bargain." Xander nodded.

"His name is Barko. He was a troll born with the Power," the wizard explained. "The mage used his Powers for evil, so the trolls banished him. Barko wanted to be human and made it his life's purpose. He would change into a man until the Power of the subterfuge ran out and then strike another bargain with a new magic wielder. The hermit may be many things, but he always kept his word. He knew his reputation would be tarnished if he broke oath.

"Many humans and trolls made bargains with him over the centuries. Barko had difficulty sustaining his transformation, so he studied Dark Arts to provide more enticing bargains. He captured foul creatures that lived in those remote areas for experimentation and sacrifice. Wandering trolls who dared enter that region never returned. He used them to gain knowledge of the Dark Arts. Safe passage was only given to those who sought bargains. Legend has it General Morgo gave up much for his dark abilities."

"He's actually a snake now," Chip said, "Oh, and he's dead." The wizard's eyes widened as Chip recounted Morgo's dark abilities.

"That explains much," Xander said as if to himself. He looked at the boy in amazement. "It took you only moments to read all those memories, which I suspect has to do with your mastery of the Calm and possibly something else." He shook his head. "If what you say of the general is true, then we have much to fear. We are both weakened considerably, and Morgo is strengthening as we speak. How do you kill what is dead?"

"You chop it into little pieces," answered Chase cheerfully, squeezing his sword hilt. "Or burn it to ash." He smiled, pleased with himself.

The wizard gave him a withering glare. "Easier said than done. It is difficult to get close to him. A regular sword will likely have no effect. Arrows fall to the ground. He covers himself with a dark energy shield, protecting him from physical threats, including fire.

Only a long and sustained use of wizard's fire may work, and even then, I suspect only Chip is strong enough." He turned to the boy. "You used much Power to defeat the dragon. If Morgo comes, do not challenge him directly. We still do not know the limits of your magic, but Morgo at full strength will almost certainly be too strong for you now."

"I feel refreshed by Miss Owl, but I will heed your advice. However, if he threatens one of you, my rage might take over," Chip said honestly.

The wizard looked up sharply. "Rage is useful until it consumes you. Without control, it can become the enemy. Using anger to unlock your Power may be necessary, but you must master it." He paused, and his piercing eyes bore into Chip. "The Unnamed One was consumed by it."

The boy shivered and nodded.

The queen stood beside the boy and took his hands into her own. Her face was weary, but she looked at him with bright eyes. "This is a lot to put on your shoulders all at once, Chip. You have already shown incredible bravery and courage. Never forget love, which hate cannot vanquish. Even when all seems lost, there is always love and hope." She smiled, and he felt comforted.

Princess Eleanor moved forward. "We are here for you, Chip." She had a strange look in her eyes. "I believe in you." She leaned over and kissed his cheek. He blushed and tried to hide his look of surprise at her words. It was the same thing little Han had said to him. Queen Charlotte looked at her nails. There was an awkward silence.

"So, where's Rupert? I mean King Rupert," Chase asked brightly. Eleanor rolled her eyes.

"I am sure he's busy organizing things from the palace." Charlotte cleared her throat. "Perhaps it is for the best anyway." She looked away. Chase tried to keep a straight face. The princess elbowed him.

Xander coughed, hiding a smirk. He beckoned his Protector, who was coordinating the rebuilding of the barricade. "Let us send out a trusted scout to see what those foul creatures are up to in the forest."

The weapons master nodded. "Oh, and he must volunteer as it will be very dangerous. The Dark Elves will kill him on sight."

Garth departed and began conversing with several soldiers. A few raised their hands, and then a young man walked back with him to the gate. The commander signalled to bring a horse forward. Xander met them in front of the smouldering pile. He asked for the soldier's shield and placed one hand on it. The wizard's eyes blazed, and Chip could see the shield glow with blue magic. The soldier then bowed and mounted his horse. Two guards moved some material aside, allowing the man to ride through the opening where the gates once stood. He rode at a light canter towards the forest.

Chip and the others stood atop the wall, watching the soldier grow smaller. It was now midafternoon, and the sun was starting to fall towards the west. The man rode towards it, casting a long shadow. Above him loomed the two distant peaks forming the Pass of Death. As his body became smaller, it seemed like little hope was left for humankind.

The enormity of what was coming struck the boy. They had defeated a few hundred demons and stayed the hand of General Morgo, yet what would happen when faced with a hundred thousand? Add to that the Dark Elves, the Inner Circle, and the Unnamed One. For a moment, Chip felt like he was on a precipice, about to take an unimaginable fall. The orphan steadied himself and focused on the disappearing soldier. The lone scout was now a tiny form on the horizon approaching a force so evil that even assuming any measure of hope might be in vain. The frustration he felt began to simmer into a rage.

Chip thought of Farn and Sally and how their lives had been extinguished in the blink of an eye. He knew that the whole city would eventually be destroyed, and there was likely nothing he could do about it, even with his Power. The Wall appeared in his mind, and he wanted to crush it, seize his magic, and unleash it upon his enemies.

But not yet. The boy knew that he must be patient. He had trained for many years with the weapons master and knew that success did not materialize overnight. He turned from the Wall in his mind and instead settled in the Calm.

Suddenly, he sensed something at a great distance. He looked around. Xander had noticed it as well and was peering intently at the forest.

"He's coming back!" shouted one of the soldiers on the wall.

"Yes, I see him!" said another.

The scout was riding hard from the direction of the forest. His horse was in full gallop with the soldier bent low over the top. Nothing materialized to pursue him, and he managed to make it across the field to the road leading up to the gates. Glancing behind him again, the young man finally slowed his horse and entered the city through a temporary opening in the debris pile. The weapons master waved him to the top of the wall. He sprinted up the steps two at a time, then saluted when he reached the top, breathing hard.

"Report, Scout Collins." Garth waited.

"The small forest was empty, sir, so I left my horse and snuck to the other side." The young soldier gulped, and his face went white. "Another army of demons has joined them. And something else."

"How many?" the commander asked calmly.

"At least equal to the original force. Five hundred for sure."

"And what else?"

Scout Collins's voice shook. "The demons were all looking behind them at something coming down the valley slope. It was shaking the very trees. I waited to see what it was. The trees kept moving until finally, a massive head broke through that looked like an armadillo but a hundred times larger. A Dark Elf woman rode the creature. She wore a blue cloak with a sword across her back. The demon beast she rode moved forward, bending the trees until its body pushed through.

"It has four huge, crooked legs on each side of its torso, covered in grey scales like armour. I do not know what could stop such a thing. It was at least fifty feet long. I tried to withdraw, but a demon sentry approached me from the side. He was only a few feet tall and quiet as a whisper. The little demon let out a shriek that alerted the main army. I returned to my horse, and when I turned around, a group of those Dark Elves had bunched together and thrown a ball of green fire at me. I blocked it with my shield, leapt on my horse, and took off."

He stopped, awaiting the commander's response.

"You did well. Your bravery is commendable. It was a risky mission, and I am pleased you returned to report." Garth saluted, and the soldier thanked him.

Before leaving, Scout Collins turned to Xander. "Whatever you did to that shield stopped that fireball. It saved my life. Thank you."

The wizard waved him off. "No need to thank me, my boy. I figured you might need a little extra protection. I am happy they stopped at one fireball. I am not sure the shield could handle two. You would likely be dead. Moreover, you would also be dead if the Dark Elf woman threw her fireball. Then, of course, if General Morgo was there and used his dark magic on you.... Well, you get the point."

The soldier's eyes widened, and he gulped. Saluting, he went back to his post, white-faced. Everyone else stared at the wizard.

"Um, how are we supposed to defeat a huge eight-legged demon armadillo that can move trees?" Chase asked casually.

"I suppose feeding you to it might only slow it down," the wizard grunted. Chase feigned terror, clutching at his heart. Chip had to grin.

Xander ignored the tall boy, turning to look at the forest in the distance.

"We will have to come up with something, but my greater concern is the rider. Her name is Marta. She is part of the Unnamed One's Inner Circle. If I recall correctly, she is a cousin of the royal family. In the Elf Wars, she was cunning and merciless. Marta is a Blue Level in magic and uses her considerable Power wisely.

"This armadillo demon will be difficult to kill. The Dark Elves have had three thousand years to cultivate creatures, each more terrible than the last. If large demons are bred with each other, each successive generation becomes bigger. Eventually, a demon, such as this armadillo, is possible. It likely has thick skin or armour that repels arrows. Tell your archers to aim for its eyes. If the demons break through the gates, we fall back to the main square barricade and, if necessary, the palace walls.

"We can slow down this monster," the commander said. He yelled at a group of soldiers fortifying the barricade. "Pour pitch all over the road leading up to the gates. Let's see if the beast can handle fire."

Chip turned to Princess Eleanor. "If they break through, get back to the palace immediately." She started to protest, but he cut her off. "I can't risk something happening to you. Please stay safe." The pleading look in his eyes gave her pause.

She smiled. "I am going to the palace now to update the king. I will return to help where needed. I will stay safe," she assured him. She gave the boy a hug and left the wall. Chip breathed a sigh of relief.

Men proceeded to douse the road with pitch. The soldiers strengthened and fortified the barricade with new furniture and metal. Extra items stood on the side to refortify the pile if it burned down. Two hours passed, and the sun began to disappear between the two peaks that formed the Pass of Death.

Dark clouds emerged from the west, their undersides glowing an ominous orange. Everything was deathly silent, and then an ill wind picked up. It was a cold breeze blowing in from the peaks, carrying a long, melancholic wail. Some men began muttering to themselves. A sense of unease permeated the air.

Something was coming.

A horn sounded, signalling the alarm. Shouts rang up and down the wall. Men pointed at the forest. It was hard to make out, but the trees at the back were swaying. A hush fell over Vanalon as the soldiers watched in awe. The forest itself was moving. The trees near the front began to wave and buckle. Cracking sounds reverberated across the fields. With a vast ripple, the forest swayed and finally opened to reveal a monstrosity.

It was two stories tall and almost as wide. The demon creature seemed to emerge from the woods without end. Even as the light waned, they could make out multiple tree-trunk-like legs carrying the massive grey bulk of its cylindrical body. As the monster left the forest, it revealed a long, serrated tail. On both sides of the beast, demons poured out of the trees, shrieking and hollering in excitement. Though distant, the inhuman sounds from the multitude rang clear. Dark, dancing bodies moved grotesquely in the deepening dusk. The wails and shrieks carried across the field, making some men turn white.

"Stand fast, men!" shouted the commander. "We defeated them once and can do so again. Harden your hearts and remember your oath. Archers, be ready. Aim for the eyes of the beast."

The horde lined up and then moved forward, with the giant demon leading the way. Sitting astride the monster was a straight-backed figure covered in a blue cloak. She held the creature's reins in red, gloved hands. The horde proceeded down the road leading to the broken gates. Nearing the city walls, just out of bowshot, the Dark Elf woman raised one hand. The entire army halted, forming a line.

The men lit extra torches and threw them in front of the walls to see their attackers, carefully avoiding the road. In the illumination, Chip roughly counted over seven hundred demons. The varied forms of creatures on the front lines were terrifying. Some new ones appeared with disturbing shapes. The demons quieted until an eerie, unnatural silence settled over everything.

"It's good to see you again, Xandrostika," Marta called, removing her blue hood to reveal a beautiful elven face with long, black hair. She smiled, showing perfect white teeth that gleamed in the torchlight. The woman was stunning, but the black almond eyes indicated she had fallen prey to the Power. "My cousin wishes to meet with you."

Her voice carried clear across the intervening space, and a gust of wind followed, pungent with the reek of demon sweat. The men wrinkled their noses, and a few gagged.

"Hello, Marta," Xander said warmly, feigning a magnanimous smile. "I see you have replaced General Morgo. Is he not feeling well?" A flash of anger swept across her face, replaced an instant later with serene calmness.

"General Morgo will join us later. He was put in an unexpected situation when one of our trusted Inner Circle failed us." She reached back to grasp a black bag. Marta brought it forward then used her other hand to remove what looked like a ball. She reached back and flung it forward. The object struck the road and rolled in front of the gates. When it stopped, the men realized it was a head. Vacant black eyes stared up at them from the half-melted face of Elohan.

Marta spat, "My Master does not like failure. The black dragon was more valuable than that fool. Morgo made sure he understood that before the end. Elohan miscalculated, and it cost him dearly." She looked around, and her eyes locked on the orphan. Chip could feel the intensity of her gaze. He wrapped himself in the Calm.

"Who is this boy?"

Xander stepped forward in front of Chip. "I am afraid that is no concern of yours. I recommend you take your horde back to Demon Island, where you belong. The land of Amrika is ours. If you continue to advance, we will destroy you this time."

A long musical laugh came out of Marta's throat. Some of the more intelligent demons chortled. "You are in no position to make threats. The great wizards are long gone. Arkan's sacrifice only bought you time. You and your brother are all that remain. The Wizard's Guild is weak and filled with Lower Levels. The so-called Light Elves have fled, realizing that humankind is a scourge on the Earth, which they want no part of. Even if you find the orb, it will not be enough. Your last shred of hope is this boy who has the red magic. He shows promise but is now weakened from the day's events. Even the Red has limits. Our Master, may we grovel at his leisure, learned how to make himself stronger than all. We are simply preparing the way so he does not need to stoop to clear the rabble in his path."

Xander stood tall. "The Unnamed One is a misguided Dark Elf taught black magic from a creature with no soul. His obsession with the Power will consume him and his evil minions. Your darkness cannot extinguish the light of the Creator. The Dark Elves have lost their way. Your foul lineage will die in disgrace."

Marta's face visibly contorted, and this time, she could not contain her rage. The demons in the front ranks growled in fury, tensing their deformed muscles. The Dark Inner Circle Elf's eyes blazed blue, and her words dripped with malice.

"You dare insult our king, the highest of the high. The barrier is all but fallen, and the earth will shake from his footsteps." She rose up and stood on the black stirrups. The beast below her whined in anticipation. "Your meddling cost us three thousand years, Orb Stealer. The world will fall under my Master's shadow. Your strength is nearly gone, wizard. I, with my pets, will destroy this human city and kill every last one of you." Marta leaned forward and patted the monstrosity beneath her. "Feast," she purred.

The armadillo demon lurched forward with a bellow. Four immense trunk-like legs moved in unison on each side. The horde kept pace with it, letting out whoops and shrieks as they eyed the men on the walls. The soldiers tried not to balk as the sun dipped below the horizon. Night had fallen.

7

"Uh, if you were trying to get them mad, it worked," Chase observed.

Xander eyed the horde. "She could have waited for more reinforcements or others from the Inner Circle. Marta could even have paused until Morgo recovered. I need her to attack now to give us a chance. Her dialogue was designed to assess our defences. In her mind, we are weak right now, but she was not sure. Her rage made the choice for her."

"So, we are not weak then?" Chase asked, a little confused.

The wizard shrugged and looked at him. "We are going to find out."

"Archers, fire at will!" the commander bellowed. Volleys of arrows rained down on the demon's front lines. Dozens fell, howling in pain, immediately replaced by those behind. The horde kept the line straight, not daring to go ahead of Marta. The traps and pits were open and easy to avoid. The archers continued raining their deadly missiles.

The enormous beast neared the formidable mound of debris where the gates once stood. It sported two immense curved tusks over ten feet long and thick as trees. The armadillo demon lowered its head, preparing to charge.

"Strike the eyes," shouted Garth. Arrows flew into the face of the beast, but a blue wall suddenly appeared, shielding the creature's head. Marta's eyes crackled brightly as she maintained the shield in front of her monstrous pet.

Xander lifted his arms. "Aim for the eyes once I attack."

The weapons master relayed the message, which passed down the line. With a sizzling jolt, a stream of blue fire shot from his hands towards Marta.

The woman was already turning to counter his strike, but in doing so, the blue shield in front of the creature's face wavered and disappeared. A dozen arrows struck its face, several landing in each eye. Marta screamed and unleashed an immense fireball in retaliation at Xander, who created a thick shield of Power.

"Duck," he called as the ball of magic exploded into his shield, which wavered but absorbed it. Xander took in a deep breath from the expenditure. They looked down and saw the armadillo demon bellowing in anger and pain as its eyes became pincushions. Marta's face was rigid with rage as she tried to control the beast thrashing violently in front of the gates.

"Light the pitch!" Garth yelled. Several soldiers threw torches from the wall onto the road slick with black goo. An explosion of flames erupted down the path like fiery creatures darting straight towards Marta. The Dark Elf straightened and wrapped herself in a blue aura of Power. The fire rushed under the armadillo and continued into the main demon horde behind her. Agonizing screams filled the night air. Those on the wall could feel the heat from the intense flames. The soldiers had to shield their eyes from the bright light.

Wrapped in her blue shield, Marta tried to maintain control of the blind creature now surrounded by red-hot flames. It performed a grotesque dance as each leg moved up and down out of sequence. She leaned down and sent a tendril of magic into the beast's head. It paused for a moment, then all its limbs went still. By now, the flames were burning the demon's whole body. Leaning its ravaged head down on the ground, it rested both tusks on the fiery road.

Then, with an ear-splitting guttural roar, the demon raised those tusks and charged forward, its fiery legs moving in tandem. Marta sat on top, linked to its brain by a flow of blue Power. The demon horde ran behind as the flames died down. This time, nothing could stop the fiery beast's momentum. It built an incredible speed and slammed into the mound of debris like a battering ram.

Furniture and chunks of metal exploded outwards, striking several men unfortunate enough to be within range. Two died instantly as pieces of metal took off their heads.

The armadillo demon's flaming body lit the rest of the debris pile, causing an inferno of fire. Men on the wall nearest the pile ran sideways to escape the incredible heat. Chip and the rest shuffled backwards to avoid the flames.

Incredibly, through the fire, Marta held on to her blue aura of Power and seemed undamaged. The armadillo's tusks had now turned black from the flames, but somehow it still lived. The creature's armour-like skin and the constant flow of Power into its brain kept it moving. With great sweeping motions, the demon brushed the pile of flaming debris out of the way, using its monstrous tusks to clear a path for the demon horde.

It started slowing down as the heat of the flames melted through its armour. The great demon began to falter. Marta pulled hard on the reins, and the beast lumbered backwards out of the hole. It stood for a moment, and then an enormous thud sounded as the great body fell to the earth one last time. The huge head sank, never to rise again. Marta leapt off its back and stood beside the flaming road, wrapped in her protective Power. She had a look of satisfaction on her face. The beast had cleared the barricade as intended. The demon army stood behind her, waiting for the last of the flames to die so they could rush the city.

"Keep firing," ordered the commander. Scores of demons fell as the arrows rained down. Marta signalled, and a group of Dark Elves came from behind the horde in a tightly knit group. A stream of green magic flew from their outstretched hands, negating the flames on the road. Their Power hit the remaining debris pile, extinguishing it.

Chip watched in anguish as the horde moved forward to enter the city, fearing what would happen. The boy's frustration fueled his rage, and he instinctively broke through the Wall in his mind.

"Not yet. They are too far," Xander tried to say, but it was too late.

Chip unleashed a red fireball at the group of Dark Elves, who shrank back in fear. They tried to erect a green shield, but the red Power sliced through it like paper, striking those in the center, killing them instantly and throwing the others outwards with explosive force. The boy turned his attention to Marta and unleashed another ball of red fire that hurtled towards her.

He knew her shield could not withstand such force. Yet as it struck, she had already moved with uncanny physical speed and was now on the other side of the road. The ball of fire landed on the empty spot where she had stood, creating a crater that knocked a chunk of the demon army backwards off their feet.

"Enough!" Xander commanded. "She is draining you of your Power. Her skill is her speed and cunning. Save your strength. She has used up some Power to control her beast but is still very dangerous. She always conserves enough for the kill."

Chip nodded as a wave of weariness washed over him. He realized she was baiting them. He vowed to be more prudent next time.

The demons surged forward.

"Form the phalanx!" Garth commanded, and thirty men filled the hole created by the armadillo demon. The ones in front kneeled and erected shields while those behind stood with spears, ready to impale any creature that came close. The demon army moved forward as one. Their losses from the arrows were heavy. Some had at least one sticking out of them. Unfortunately, that still left over half the demon army trying to enter the city unscathed or slightly injured.

"Archers, continue firing until there's a breach," Garth commanded. He ran down the stairs as the first wave slammed against the phalanx. The men with the shields grunted from the weight of demon bodies. The soldiers standing behind them struck anything within reach. Chip watched as spears impaled the creatures through their eyes or fanged mouths then jutted out the backs of their heads. As they fell, the demons behind crawled over them.

At first, it looked like the phalanx would hold, but claws continued to get through, raking the men holding the shields. Some demons with strong hands grasped the spears and yanked the men forward to sink hungry fangs into their necks. Screams erupted from the injured soldiers, and the phalanx began to waver.

"Replace them!" Garth shouted above the din. The injured men were pulled out, and fresh ones were inserted in the holes. The number of dead demons in the front began to pile up to the point where it was difficult for the creatures behind to climb over them. This helped form a barricade.

Suddenly, several spider-like demons leapt atop the mound and sprang over the entire phalanx. One judged its jump too short, and three spears impaled its fat body. The others landed behind the soldiers and ran at anything in sight. Chase pulled his sword, as did the weapons master. They ran down the stairs and became blurs of motion, slicing off legs and antennae at will. The others followed to lend support.

A particularly large spider demon charged towards Chase and leapt completely over him. Chip stepped in front of Queen Charlotte, sword at the ready. The creature snaked out its front two legs, trying to wrench the boy towards its mandibles. The demon's eyes showed intelligent calculation, and he realized it was targeting him. He used his shimmering elven blade to chop its lead leg off, then slice through both mandibles on the upswing. Chase whirled to attack its hind legs from the back. Another soldier tried to jump in and slice its body, but he was too slow and overextended himself. The creature flailed one of its legs sidewise, sweeping its talon across the man's stomach, spilling his innards onto the cobblestone. As he sank to his knees, the leg whipped back to decapitate him. Chip leapt forward in retaliation, using a two-handed overhead blow to cleave its triangular head in two. The creature's body crashed to the ground as it died. He looked at the dead soldier with regret and wondered if he should have used his Power to kill the demon. If so, the soldier would still be alive.

Xander looked at him in understanding. "It is a curse of the Power that you must always carry, Chip. If you use too much to save a few, you risk dying and losing many. Always seek to conserve, and you can live to fight another day. Before this battle is over, you will have wished you had conserved more."

The wizard turned as the soldiers in front began to shout.

Several heavily muscled demons were tossing the dead bodies from the pile straight at the phalanx, creating chaos. Each time the men tried to reform, another body came hurtling at them with bone-crushing force.

"Archers!" shouted the commander. "Target them." Garth pointed at the muscular demons that were tossing their dead brethren around like leaves. At that moment, a line of blue fire swept across the top of the wall, severing the heads of a dozen archers. The rest ducked in fear. Cursing, Xander climbed up the stairs to counter Marta's attack. He halted on the landing at the halfway point and turned to look at the chaos below him. Extending both arms, the wizard unleashed a vicious stream of blue fire into the midst of the muscular demons. Several had dead bodies in their hands and tried to use them as shields with limited success. The fire melted the bodies into hot wax that fell on the faces of the muscular ones and burnt their hands. The ones that survived screamed and ran back into the horde.

"Archers, shoot from here instead. It's safer," ordered Xander. The landing he stood on midway up the wall provided enough space for several men to keep firing. The phalanx regrouped as a fresh wave of demons attacked the shields, scratching and biting anything they could touch. The men began to show signs of exhaustion.

"Relieve them," Garth ordered, inserting a new group of soldiers. They managed to repel the attacks for a while, but the weight of the demon's advance was relentless. The front line began to move backwards. Soon, the horde would have enough space on the sides to pour through. The wounds began to mount until most of the men had some injury, from minor to serious.

"Hold!" shouted the commander.

The attack stopped without warning. A few men let out hoarse cheers. Garth knew better. "Hold steady!"

Rushing feet sounded on the demon side, and the soldiers in the front braced themselves with resigned looks. Two dozen spider demons skittered up the sides of the pile of dead bodies, launching themselves onto and over the phalanx. At the same time, muscular demons appeared, this time throwing live bodies into the phalanx.

"To the gates!" shouted the weapons master to all the remaining soldiers in the city. Everyone ran forward to repel the concerted attack. The men fought bravely, but one by one, they began to fall. The demons were too many. Xander, dishevelled, ran back up to the landing and unleashed a stream of crackling blue magic into the enemy. A dozen of them dissolved into what looked like melted wax. For a moment, it seemed like the men would hold, but a loud bellow echoed outside the gates, giving everyone pause.

"What now?" muttered Chase, holding his sword high.

In answer, a fifteen-foot-long solid block of muscle and fury ran full force into the phalanx, destroying it in one fell swoop. Men flew sideways as it careened through them. When the monster finally stopped, it turned, and the sight of it made most of the soldiers balk. It was a creature built from top to bottom for destruction.

The massive head resembled an ox with large knobs of bone protruding to form a square that looked like it could batter through the city wall itself. The body had disproportionate shoulders and upper leg muscles meant to push forward through any object. Serrated bone, looking sharper than knives, covered the beast from head to toe. The eyes were set deep and surrounded by spurs for protection.

Marta had been saving this for last.

The ox demon ran through the phalanx like parchment and then stood in the square, searching for its next target. At that unfortunate moment, Princess Eleanor appeared around the corner, returning from the palace. She saw Chip first, and her face lit up, but then her eyes took in the demon ox, which lined up in front of her. She was dressed in red. The beast locked onto her like a beacon.

It lowered its head and charged at the princess.

Everyone was too far away to intervene in time. Chip watched as the monster bore down on Eleanor. She cried out in fear and defiantly pulled out a small dagger. The small girl stood alone. The boy's frustration turned to rage, which swept over him. Chip smashed through the Wall in his mind and threw his Power at the beast in the shape of a red hand. Sadly, he knew the hand would not reach her in time.

Eleanor saw his attempt to help and scrambled backwards to give him more time. In doing so, she tripped and fell down. Seeing her fall, the ox demon paused at the end of its charge to leap up and bring its head down to crush her. That slight hesitation was all Chip needed. As the knobby bones touched her chest, the red hand of Power seized the creature and lifted it impossibly high in the air. It shrank in size as it flew to an unbelievable height, and then the boy brought it back down to smash on the cobblestones with an impact that shook the ground. Nothing could survive such force. The beast broke inside its skin like a bag of brittle bones and remained unmoving in a jumbled heap. It was not even recognizable anymore.

The spider-like demons hissed with rage and ran at Chip, but he turned and dispatched them with lancing bolts of red fire. For a moment, a wave of exhaustion rocked him, and he nearly stumbled.

"Chip, watch out!"

From the corner of his eye, the boy saw a massive ball of blue fire coming from Marta's direction. It struck him in the back as he tried to leap away. Before it hit him, he sensed Xander trying to cover him with a shield, but it only partially blocked the impact. The force sent the orphan hurtling through a shop window, where he crashed into furniture before striking the back wall.

Chip's vision went black and then reappeared hazy and strange. Sounds dulled, and he heard a ringing. His back burned terribly, and he scrambled to try to pull off his shirt, but it was stuck to him. The boy clutched for his Power, but the searing pain created fear, and the Wall materialized. He felt a sharpness in his chest.

Then, someone was by his side. He could not make out the face and, for a fleeting moment, thought it was a demon about to tear him apart as he lay helpless. The face crystallized into the princess.

"Dear Creator, you are alive," she cried, holding his head. "You must try to get up. They are coming. They've breached the gates." She pulled him into a sitting position, which sent waves of pain and exhaustion through him. He looked at her consternation and gritted his teeth, trying to stand up. Things felt broken in him, but he pushed forward. Eleanor put his arm over her shoulders, causing him to cry out, then half-dragged the boy out the back of the store into an alley. As they exited, something crashed into the store.

"Fall back!" the weapons master shouted in the distance. A demonic whine sounded from the direction of the store as they struggled down the alley. Sounds of items being smashed followed them, and then one of the spider demons burst through the back door into the alleyway. It saw them and shrieked with glee. Eleanor pulled her knife out and stood in front of Chip, face resolute.

"You can't have him," she screamed. Chip's fury ignited at the thought of the creature attacking her, and he broke through his Wall. He reached for his Power as the demon prepared to spring forward. The boy saw his magic as a pool of red Power in his mind. Behind it, he could see a white ball of energy for the first time.

At that moment, he knew it was his spirit essence. He remembered Xander discussing how his father Arkan used it to create the barrier. It was the ultimate sacrifice. Chip knew he was drawing on the limits of his magic if he could see his spirit essence. He drew from the red Power around it, and his mind cleared.

"Duck," he ordered, his voice infused with raw Power. She dropped to the ground without hesitation, and he unleashed a line of red fire straight at the demon as it leapt forward. The thing disintegrated into a puddle of melted flesh at their feet.

Eleanor started pulling Chip down the alley as more demons emerged from the back of other stores. He dispatched them with bursts of magic. Waves of weariness struck the boy, and the pain returned, even while he held on to the Power. Chip knew he was in dire trouble.

Marta had cleverly timed her attack on him after sending the fearsome ox demon into their midst. She had used the all-out assault to occupy him so he would use his magic and be vulnerable from behind. She was cunning, as Xander had warned.

Three more demons piled in from side alleys, and he knew the game was up. The magic started to fizzle, and his sight grew blurry. Eleanor's breath behind him laboured as she dragged him foot by foot. Both felt exhausted. He sent one final slice of red fire across the necks of the three demons before him and watched as their heads fell off. His hand dropped. Blackness started forming at the edge of his vision, and he fell on his back, sending more pain everywhere. He had at least cleared the alley of demons. Chip heard the princess collapse behind him, breathing raggedly. She could pull him no further without resting.

Without a sound, something emerged around the corner of the side alley they had just passed. It was only three feet tall. A short dark cloak covered its small body. The piercing black almond eyes in its wizened face looked vicious and intelligent.

It was an assassin demon.

The small creature drew a short black knife and held it in its tiny, clenched hand. The demon analyzed their predicament, seeming to assess the risk. Chip felt it had been waiting all along for such a moment, a final gift from Marta. It walked forward on silent feet. The boy raised his hand weakly, but no magic came forth. The Wall popped back up in his mind.

The orphan looked at certain death, and this time, he could not say no. A fear entered him not just for himself but also for the princess. She was too weak to defend herself. It walked up and stepped onto his chest. He gasped in pain.

A smile of pure evil crossed the demon's face. The assassin looked him dead in the eyes as it swiped the small knife sideways across his throat in a blur of motion and looked down to watch him bleed out.

Yet no blood came. A puzzled look crossed its face, which turned into shock and then pain as a fountain of black blood pumped out of its severed wrist. Eleanor sat behind Chip, her short dagger dripping. The creature screamed, realizing what she had done, then watched as she swiped the knife again, slicing its throat wide open. Black blood sprayed them as it fell backwards, gurgling in its death throes.

"You cannot have him," she croaked to the dead assassin. The princess took a couple of deep breaths and started pulling on him again. Pain wracked Chip's body and mind. He wanted to give up, but the weapons master's voice echoed in his head.

"The one rule above them all, never give up!"

He pulled his sword out and pushed himself to his feet, using it as a crutch. His body protested. Pain exploded from everywhere. Chip grunted and nearly vomited. Eleanor inserted herself under his arm, and they turned down the alley towards the city's center.

Behind them, a spider demon burst forth from the same alley as the assassin. They did not turn in time. Two claws raked into his back. He could barely feel it. The boy swung his sword backwards, but it ducked under and opened its mandibles to sever his head. Eleanor distracted the demon with a strike, and it reared back instead, but a taloned front leg whipped around and slashed her across the thigh. Chip's vision swam, but he stuck his sword arm out anyway, keeping it at bay. Even that was a struggle to maintain, and his arm fell of its own accord.

He tried again, but nothing responded. In slow motion, the orphan saw the demon crouch and open its mandibles, revealing two sharp fangs. The creature sprang forward to sever his head at the neck.

Out of nowhere, a figure appeared behind it with raised arms and drove a sword through the top of its head, killing the beast instantly. It was Chase. He freed his blade, and the demon's body dropped to the stones in front of them. Chip was never so happy to see anyone in his life. His best friend stood covered in black blood. "There you are. I've been looking all over for you," Chase grinned fiendishly. Chip tried to smile but could not. "The city is overrun. Let's get behind the barricade in the main square while we still can. You don't look so good, Chip. This is going to hurt."

Chase sheathed his sword, grabbed his best friend under his knees and elbows, and lifted him over his shoulder. The tall boy dashed down the alley as if the orphan was a feather. Fresh pain coursed through Chip. He struggled to reach the Calm in his mind but could not. Eleanor ran raggedly beside them.

They had to backtrack twice through side alleys as they heard demons approaching, but they finally reached the square and the first barricade. A small group of demons were already assaulting it. Xander stood on the other side, and a look of great relief crossed his face as he saw them approach. The wizard unleashed a stream of blue fire at the demons in front, scattering the whole group and allowing the three to run through a small opening the soldiers had created.

Chase laid Chip on the ground, and the wizard knelt beside him.

"He has broken ribs, burns, deep cuts, and is near exhaustion. Can you help?" Xander looked at Queen Charlotte, who rushed up with concern. She nodded and placed both hands on his chest. The boy's vision blurred with pain. Then, a warm feeling entered his body, and the broken things inside seemed to fall back into place. The pain subsided considerably, and he could breathe again. His back felt better, too, though it remained sore. His vision cleared.

"Thank you," he gasped in relief. Queen Charlotte removed her hands and sat back, exhausted. Dark circles appeared under her eyes.

"It is the least I can do," she said and turned to her daughter.

"It's alright. I can manage." Eleanor objected as the queen tried to heal her. "You have done more than enough. Conserve your strength for those who need it. Thank you." Someone offered her a bandage, and she wrapped her leg. Queen Charlotte nodded and rose unsteadily to her feet.

"Thanks, Chase." Chip smiled at his friend. You could not have come at a better time...Well, other than earlier."

Chase laughed. "It's the least I could do after you threw that ox demon into the sky. I would have had trouble with that one."

Chip looked around and saw how few soldiers were left defending the barricade. "What happened?" he asked Xander, who stood by with a strange look on his face.

The wizard shook his head. "You amaze me, boy. Destroying that ox creature was quite a feat. Marta waited for you to expend your energy and be distracted before she pounced. I tried to throw up a shield, but it only blocked some of the force and heat. I had to fend her and the other demons off before I could reach you. She retreated behind the horde as they poured in. The men fought bravely, but we could not make it to the store in time. There were too many pushing us backwards down the main avenue. It was Chase's idea to try to find you through the alley system, but even that began to be overrun by demons. I stayed to protect the remaining soldiers and allow them to get behind this barricade. I was waiting here to create an opening for you. I must say, after the impact of that fireball, I had serious concerns. You expended great energy saving the princess from that ox, but it was well worth it." He put his hand on the boy's shoulder and smiled.

"I would do it all over again," Chip responded. Princess Eleanor blushed. "Besides, I wouldn't be here without her."

The wizard nodded before grimacing. "I am afraid we are in a tough situation. Well over half our men are dead, and many of the remaining soldiers are injured. Our use of the Power has weakened us considerably, leaving little for reserve. Over two hundred demons are still alive, a few Dark Elves, and Marta. We do not stand a chance one-on-one. We must retreat to the palace."

Even as he spoke, sounds of alarm rang out as the barricade began to crumble. A dozen archers were firing at will, but their quivers were almost empty. A spurt of green fire hit the barricade, and an explosion of wood showered them all. A large hole opened in the middle.

"Phalanx, plug the hole!" ordered the commander. "Everyone else, retreat to the palace." Demons of all shapes and sizes began to run through the opening. The shield men dropped in formation in front of the spear wielders. It was apparent they would not hold long.

"Captain Mac, douse the rest with pitch and light her up!" The captain nodded and ordered two men to grab the large buckets at either end of the pile and empty them over the structure.

The fire would give the men in the phalanx time to retreat once everyone else had fallen back. Chip stretched his arms and legs. He ached everywhere but felt much better. Being able to take deep breaths felt wonderful.

"Wait with me until the others are safe," Xander instructed the boys. The princess hugged him and left with the queen and the remaining soldiers. Captain Mac grabbed a torch and prepared to light the barricade. As he stepped forward, several giant spider demons leapt over the others and landed on the phalanx. At the same time, a small but powerful ox-like beast rammed the shield men, forcing a line straight through. It was much smaller than the one at the gates but still incredibly powerful.

The beast struck Captain Mac as he was about to throw the torch. The weapons master dodged to the side to avoid the same fate and twisted simultaneously, holding his sword tight. As the demon hit the captain, Garth swung down with all his might, cleaving halfway through its neck. Unfortunately, its front tusks had gored the captain's stomach and remained caught in his rib cage.

The torch flew out of Mac's hand. The ox-like demon thrashed violently, and even Garth had to step back. Chip ran forward and raised his hands, but Xander grabbed him.

"It's too late. The captain is already dead. Grab the torch and light the barricade!"

He urged the boy forward then turned to face a tall, sinewy demon that had slipped through. The ox was in its death throes and finally fell on its side. The captain's body still hung on its tusks, ripped to shreds. The whole phalanx broke apart, with demons pouring through multiple holes.

The weapons master, cold steel in his eyes, was a blur of motion as three spider demons surrounded him. Limbs and appendages flew into the air as he carved his way through. Chip saw the torch off to the side and dove for it. Grasping it in his right hand, he rolled and regained his feet, then threw it over the entire melee into the barricade.

There was a huge flash of light and heat as the entire pile ignited from end to end. The demons trapped on the palace side screamed at the bright light, and the men took advantage. He remembered the wizard's warning to conserve his magic. The boy used his sword instead to deliver death to the creatures before him.

The soldiers, raging at the loss of their captain, fought like madmen and cut down the remaining demons. Garth himself dispatched a large number that were foolish enough to come within reach. A mound of bodies surrounded the weapons master. He stepped over a corpse in front of him and sheathed his sword.

The barricade was a bright flaming light that kept the demons at bay for the moment. Over half of the phalanx was dead.

"Retreat to the palace," the commander ordered. The survivors nodded with weariness. Garth looked at Xander. "Captain Mac will receive a proper burial if we get through this." The wizard nodded. The man's corpse was almost sundered in two and still entangled in the ox's tusks.

The survivors moved quickly to vacate the square while the fire still raged, knowing it would soon burn out, allowing the horde through. They could hear the mewls and whines of the demons on the other side as they smelled burnt man flesh.

The defenders raced through the deserted city to the castle gates. There was a park-like area in front of the palace that would give them ample view of the demon army. The walls, however, were only ten feet high, which did not inspire a lot of confidence. Some of the demons might even be able to leap over them in one bound. Chip shook his head, wondering how they would make it through. He felt like a noose was tightening around them, and soon, there would be no place to go. They crossed the park and entered the gates. The soldiers inside gave ragged cheers, which muted when they realized how few of their comrades had survived.

The commander addressed them all, "The demon army approaches. You have all fought bravely, but there is still more to do.

Remember your duties. We have defeated most of their army, but the threat remains. Understand that no matter how tired or hurt you are, you still have much in reserve. Dig deep. This will be a battle you tell your children and grandchildren. If you do not make it, we will tell it for you.

"We are defending the Kingdom of Vanalon from the biggest threat to humankind in three thousand years. It is an honour to fight beside you for the greatest of causes. If the gate falls, we retreat to the palace proper and the throne room. There, we will make our final stand. Give it everything you have and pray it will be enough. Above all, do not give up. For Vanalon!" He raised his sword high, and the men followed suit with loud cheers.

8

A sound emerged in the distance, and their shouts subsided. It was a high-pitched whine mixed with steady thumping. The noise increased in intensity, chilling the blood. The soldiers turned to see the demon horde moving down the main avenue like a roiling black ball of death. Their whines turned into wild shrieks as the palace appeared, and they spotted their prey.

The demons spilled into the park, fanning out in a long line. Their numbers were still alarming. Bodies of all shapes and sizes erupted in a revolting dance amidst the flickering torchlight. The creatures abruptly paused in unison as if from a hidden signal. The foul beasts were eager to rush forward and rend limb from limb but adhered to discipline in the presence of their masters. The center opened, and Marta walked forward imperiously with three Dark Elves on each side. The horde stood a safe distance from the metal gates. She stopped and looked up triumphantly.

"Looks like you have run out of options, Xandrostika. I sense your weakness and fear. You do not have near enough men left to resist us." She smiled, showing shiny white teeth.

"Why don't you come find out?" the wizard asked. "Your army is dwindling rapidly from our vantage point."

She let out a melodious peal of laughter. "This attack is a tiny preliminary force to test the waters. Can you imagine what one hundred thousand can do? Let alone the rest of the Inner Circle and our Master, may we grovel at his leisure. Your Powers are nearly spent. The boy is lucky to be alive. This small horde alone will be enough to destroy the great wizard who stole the orb and the boy with red eyes. My Master will be pleased, may we grovel at his leisure. You have a few dozen men who can still fight. Give it up and go down with some dignity. I will spare your lives and let the men go free. We will escort you and the boy to our glorious Master. He may even show mercy if you beg. He is fond of new pets. I can petition him to allow the two of you to serve as his slaves and keep the torture to a minimum. To be in the vicinity of his eminence is the highest honour, regardless of station. I can only offer this once."

Xander took a step forward. "Your kindness is beyond measure. That is a generous offer." Marta smiled in appreciation, happy he could finally see it was the only logical option. Her expression turned to pity, and she waited politely for his surrender. "However, I fear that we cannot accept being slaves to a creature so foul and evil that his very existence is an abomination to life itself." Marta's face recoiled in shock and rage. "With a token force of men, a boy, and an old wizard, we killed your Master's black dragon, injured his highest general, defeated Elohan, and destroyed one thousand demons. We will kill you, too, before night's end. Mark my words: by the will of the Creator, we will defend hope. Be gone, spawn of evil, or suffer the consequences."

Her mouth contorted, but no words came out. All pretense of civility was gone. She screamed at the horde. "Kill them all!"

The demons needed no further motivation. They ran forward, shrieking with glee, their black eyes full of malevolence.

"Well, that sure got them fired up," Chase remarked.

"Might have been a little excessive," the wizard admitted. "Let's hope she makes a mistake." They watched as the horde advanced.

"Man the walls!" the commander bellowed. "Archers, fire at will!"

There were only two dozen archers left who stood in single file along the thin but sturdy stone wall. Their quivers were at least full from the palace reserves. The demons crossed the park haphazardly in various modes of movement, depending on their body structure. They ran, skittered, crawled, and lumbered in macabre motions. Several of the ones in front fell as arrows pierced their dark bodies, but the rest kept coming.

Soldiers continued piling items behind the wrought iron gate to bolster it. The front ranks of the demons were almost at the wall when the earth gave way, and they fell into the dry moat on either side of the gate. Razor-sharp spikes ten feet down greeted them as they dropped in waves into the pits.

Marta shrieked in warning, and the rest of the demons stopped at the pit's edge, watching their impaled comrades struggle. The fallen creatures squirmed and howled in pain. The horde fell back on her command and reformed on the road leading to the gates. At her signal, a taller one leapt up and bounded over the gate, crashing into the pile of debris stacked against it. The soldiers dispatched it, but more kept hopping over until the pile started falling away, weakening the gates.

The archers fired rapidly as the demons bunched up in a group and ran at the gates, using sheer weight. The sound of bending metal eclipsed the shrieking of the creatures as the gates buckled inward.

Xander waited as long as he could before releasing a blazing blue fireball into the group of demons at the front, sending fiery bodies flying in all directions. As soon as he did, the Dark Elves at the back unleashed a string of green fire in retaliation. He erected a blue shield in response, which absorbed the fire. As both dissipated, Marta conjured her own fireball, which streaked towards the wizard. Xander strained to create another shield but managed to block her attack. He stepped backwards and almost fell off the wall.

"Be careful," he gasped to Chip. "Marta is timing her strikes when we are weakest." He wiped his brow. The boy knew the old man was exhausted.

A loud groan indicated the gates were tearing loose as the

demons renewed their attack. A particularly large one, grinning wolfishly in the front, placed its muscled arms on two bars.

"Push," it ordered in a deep, guttural voice. The whole gate bowed inwards, and Chip could see its muscles bulging out in knotted cords as the demon strained with all its might. The archers continued firing, but there were too many. Other larger demons rushed up and pushed on the other bars. There was an audible snap as the hinge came loose at one end, then the other, and finally, the gate fell forward, resting at an angle on the heap of debris behind it.

The large demon, now impaled with several arrows, bounded through the debris and raked the foremost soldier with its claws. The man screamed as Chase pulled him out of the way. The heavily muscled beast paused to look at the tall boy, then lifted its arms to strike. In a blur of motion, Chase sliced across its belly, then cut the thing's throat on his backhand.

The demon registered a look of surprise before its eyes rolled back and fell dead. Chase nodded to Chip, who had his sword drawn. The creatures behind screamed and pushed forward simultaneously, and the whole structure started to move forward.

"Get off the walls," ordered Garth. "Light it up."

A soldier stood off to the side with a torch raised. "Get back!" he shouted to the others. The man waited a moment and then threw the torch, igniting the pile, which engulfed several demons trying to crawl through. The weapons master strode forward and efficiently dispatched the creatures trapped on the palace side.

"Retreat to the palace!" he commanded above the din.

Everyone sprinted to the open doors of the main entrance. Chip was one of the last to enter. Looking behind, he saw that the demons had already found a gap through the burning pile and were racing full speed towards them. He slipped inside with the others and moved into the foyer. The weapons master entered last, pulling the door shut just as a speeding demon crashed into it from the other side. The commander dropped the heavy bar in place and ushered everyone down the hall.

The throne room was easily large enough to hold the forty or so survivors. Chip looked around and saw King Rupert sitting atop his throne, dressed in his best royal outfit. He even wore his crown. The young monarch's flabby face was pale, and a damp sheen of sweat dotted his forehead.

Biff, Gunter, and Chubs stood before him with swords drawn. None of them looked like they had any idea how to use them. He had never seen any of them train. It would have been comical but for the gravity of the situation. Chase's father, Squire Longfellow, stood to the side looking grave.

The high commander strode up to the throne. "King Rupert, I regret to inform you that Vanalon has fallen. We are all that remain. Your men fought bravely and will continue to fight with the possibility of victory still in their hearts. We will defend you until the end. I recommend you use the escape tunnel, and we will follow when it is safe." King Rupert gulped and nodded.

A booming sounded on the outside doors.

The weapons master looked at the men with cold steel in his eyes. "It has been an honour. I ask for your service one last time. To the doors!" He turned and left the throne room with sword in hand. The remaining soldiers, perhaps twenty men who could still fight, followed him down the hall and waited. The injured ones remained behind. The solid oak palace entrance doors had heavy metal hinges that reverberated with each rhythmic, hypnotic bang. They began to bulge and buckle inwards with every successive impact. High-pitched screeches mixed with low, heavy grunts sounded on the other side. Marta and the Dark Elves could throw a fireball and incinerate the doors, but they likely wished to conserve their magic for the end. It made more sense for them to let the demons do their bidding for now.

Chip and the others waited in the throne room. They were a ragged bunch, injured and burned. Exhaustion covered their faces. The banging on the door was like a bell of doom. King Rupert shook.

"Mother, open the tunnel," he begged.

Queen Charlotte nodded sadly and walked behind the throne. She reached under and pulled a lever beneath the chair. "Help me," she said, beginning to push sideways on the oak throne. King Rupert lumbered over but then changed his mind and ordered Gunter and Chubs to help instead. They put their shoulders into the side of the chair and moved it, slowly revealing a metal trap door. The banging at the entrance grew louder, mixed with sounds of cracking wood.

The queen stared, mesmerized. "For three thousand years, we have defended Vanalon. This escape hatch has never been used in our history." A tear rolled down her cheek.

"Just hurry up, Mum." The king pushed her out of the way, then reached down and turned the handle. He pulled, but nothing happened.

"No!" he screamed in a high-pitched voice. The king strained with all his might, his voice rising to a frantic pitch. Finally, with a groan, the trap door lifted upward, revealing a ladder leading down into a black hole. Rupert exhaled explosively and let out a relieved grin.

He pointed at Gunter and Chubs. "Go first and make sure it's alright." They ambled over and squinted down the dark shaft. Gunter put his hands on his knees and peered down. "Hurry," Rupert pushed his shoulder, and Gunter almost fell forward headfirst. Grumbling, the large young man turned around and shuffled down the ladder. His head disappeared and then came straight back up.

"I thought I heard something," Gunter said uneasily. "It's pitch black."

"Bring him a torch!" the king screamed at Chase's father. Mr. Longfellow ran to the wall and tried to remove one from the nearest sconce, but it was clamped tight. He unscrewed the bottom as fast as he could to release it. "Move it, you worthless lout. I'll have you lashed for this."

The squire gave the screw another turn then pulled the torch out and handed it to Gunter. Mr. Longfellow's face was red, but he managed to smile in deference. Chip looked over and saw Chase clenching one large fist, glowering at the king.

A splintering of wood sounded down the hall. Chase vented his anger by grabbing the dining room table and heaving it on its side, scattering the bowls of fruit and cutlery. The king looked outraged.

"What is the meaning of this?" Rupert demanded.

Chase ignored him and waved Chip over. "Help me turn the table." They pushed it broadside to face the doors leading to the throne room. The king realized what they were doing, grunted, and turned back to watch Chubs go down through the trap door after Gunter.

Suddenly, a thunderous reverberating crash echoed down the hallway as the front doors to the palace smashed inwards. Chip looked down the hall into the foyer to see six muscular demons throwing a battering ram to the side as they burst through the entrance. The weapons master stood beside the other soldiers in the narrow hallway and skewered the first two before they took three steps.

Behind them, a mass of demon bodies pushed forward, slashing and biting. Shrieks echoed down the hall.

King Rupert cried out in fear at the sight of the dark creatures. A look of horror and fright covered his pudgy face, making him look almost comical. He turned to escape down the ladder but stopped when he heard a loud, muffled shriek from the tunnel below. It sounded like Gunter.

"Is everything alright, Gunter?" he called down. The king looked around, not sure what to do. The backs of a knot of soldiers appeared in the throne room as the front line was inexorably pushed back down the hallway. The commander's sword rained death, but the confined space limited his movements. Several soldiers dropped as the demons tore at their throats and eyes. Pale-faced recruits steadfastly took their spot, but there were few men left.

King Rupert's face contorted in fear then turned resolute as he decided to risk the tunnel. He put his foot down on the first ladder rung, but another scream reverberated through the throne room. This one was definitely Chubs, and much closer.

"Close the trap door," ordered Xander. "Something is down there."

Rupert pulled his foot back and looked at the demons coming down the hall. His face twisted in anguish and uncertainty. At that moment, the rest of the soldiers spilled backwards into the throne room, unable to hold the antechamber. Two immense demons strode in, clearing the dead bodies for those behind. The men, down to a dozen, formed a semi-circle around the entrance. The others stood behind the table. Xander and Chip raised their arms, eyes crackling with magic.

Seeing the demons up close made King Rupert gasp in horror, and the terrified monarch turned to take his chance with the trap door. As he looked down, two round objects suddenly flew out of the hole, one striking the king in the face. He backed up in shock, holding his bleeding nose. Rupert looked down to see what struck him and saw the decapitated heads of Gunter and Chubs. He emitted a high-pitched scream.

Then, like a dark wraith from the netherworld, a figure emerged from the trap door wearing a midnight black hooded cloak. It climbed out and bent the very light of the room. General Morgo removed his hood. His reptilian face grinned with pure malice.

Xander's eyes crackled an intense blue while Chip's blazed bright red. They both raised their arms at the general and unleashed as one, red joining blue, in a wicked display of Power. Yet Morgo was already gone. They followed his blurring body as he raced behind the demon horde with uncanny speed.

Both severed their Power, realizing how little they had left. The battle had raged all day, and they were exhausted. A wave of weariness washed over Chip, and the wizard wobbled.

"He is not human anymore. I misjudged his speed," the wizard whispered, breathing raggedly. His eyes still blazed blue, but they were much weaker.

"I won't miss again," promised Chip. He gritted his teeth.

The two huge demons in front of the throne room doors stepped aside, revealing Morgo, who reappeared with a gloating smile. Beside him was Marta, chin lifted high in triumph. On the other side were six Dark Elves with victorious looks on their pale faces. The other demons fanned out into the throne room and then froze, awaiting their master's wishes. The creatures knew this was the end and would be feasting shortly.

Morgo stepped forward. "You are spent." His voice was a silky hiss. "You fought bravely, even for humans," he conceded. "I am, however, at my full Power again. The Dark Elves healed my wounds, and I absorbed the rest from the life around me. Even with the boy, you are not strong enough to defeat me. I offer you one last chance to live at my Master's feet. It is a great honour to spend the rest of your days in servitude to his Eminence. If you resist, I will take you anyway and subject all of you to a lifetime of unending torture. Or I can just kill you now."

He smiled grotesquely, awaiting their response. Marta shook her head in wonder at such a generous offer.

"Quick question," Chase called from the back. "If you are so powerful, then why give us a choice? Is it not easier to just take us by force and then torture us forever?" The smile vanished from Morgo's face. Marta's eyes blazed blue, but she restrained herself. "You aren't scared, are you?"

The second comment made Marta raise her hands. The general reached out and rested his hand on her arm. She slowly lowered them.

Morgo spat. "You are a human with no Power, and as such, I grant you no recognition, but I will say this: the outcome is certain. Despite that, I like to see my enemies grovel. It gives me great pleasure watching them capitulate and beg for mercy." He started to raise his hands.

"Why does your Master want to destroy the world?" Chip asked unexpectedly. Xander glanced at him, eyes calculating.

Morgo lowered his arms, considering the boy with red eyes. "The world has forsaken us. Every last human and Light Elf will die by our hand. We desire to control all the Power in the world, including what is in the Ancient City." He paused, and a look of respect crossed his features. "You ask questions even at the end. Could you possibly still have hope?" He laughed a reptilian hissing sound. "You and the

Ancient King must die, boy. Only one red-eye can open the book. Very well, death it is." Again, he started raising his hands.

"Please wait!" cried a voice in the back. Morgo turned with an irritated look.

"Who speaks?" the general hissed.

The king waved his hands. "I do. I'm King Rupert." He still wore his crown, which hung lopsided, and tears streamed down his face. His grey breeches appeared soiled with urine at the front. The king's childhood friend Biff stood next to him, slack-jawed. "I will accept the offer. Please don't kill me," Rupert cried.

Morgo gestured slightly, his black eyes blazing, and the king flew across the room to float in front of him. The general closed one hand on his throat. Rupert tried to gasp.

"No!" Queen Charlotte cried. Nobody could release their magic for fear of striking the king. Biff, holding his sword awkwardly, grunted and charged at the general. The large demon to the side leapt in front of Morgo and raked Biff with one massive claw from groin to chin.

Biff looked down with one last look of confusion; then everything spilled out of him at the same time. He sank to the floor in a heap of intestines and organs.

Morgo's reptilian face turned and studied the whimpering king for a moment. "I did not make the offer to you, weak human." He held him out to the large demon. "Feast."

The muscled creature clamped massive jaws on King Rupert's neck, tearing into his flesh. Blood sprayed sideways, and his crown fell to the floor, clanging loudly. Rupert let out one last whimper and went still.

Xander and Chip released a torrent of magic at the same time. As one, Morgo, Marta, and the Dark Elves formed an interlaced shield. As the combined red and blue Power struck it, a brief look of uncertainty crossed Morgo's features, and his face strained against the onslaught. The Dark Elves gritted their teeth as looks of consternation took hold. Marta struggled to maintain the shield. Then, the red magic went through and struck the Dark Elves first, being the weakest. They screamed as their white faces melted. The black eyes liquefied and boiled in their sockets. The screams cut short as their bodies fell to the ground in steaming husks. Marta began to shake. Morgo faltered and fell to his knees. His face held disbelief.

Then Chip felt an emptiness he had never experienced. He pulled for more Power, but there was nothing there. The red magic trailed out and disappeared. He looked sideways and saw that Xander was also spent. The wizard's blue fire died out. Blackness pushed in against Chip's vision, and exhaustion permeated every part of his being. He sank to one knee. The boy had nothing left.

Chip raised his head weakly to see Morgo standing back up and Marta beaming. Her hair was in disarray and singed at the ends, but her face had an air of victory. "You forgot to conserve, old man," she sneered, walking forward. "Not even the boy can save you now."

The woman stopped at the overturned table and raised her hands. Xander levitated off his feet. She surrounded him with a blue aura and started cooking him. His robes began to smoke. The wizard let out a low moan and thrashed weakly.

"I saved some magic," Queen Charlotte said, unleashing a thin stream of yellow fire straight at Marta. A look of shock crossed the Dark Inner Circle Elf's face as she barely shielded herself in time. Xander dropped to the floor in a heap. Marta grunted but was clearly stronger. She nullified the yellow magic, then sent a stream of compressed air at Charlotte. The queen flew back and struck the wall hard. The elf strode up to her with a look of rage. The general watched from a distance with an evil grin.

"You dare attack me with your pathetic Powers, weak human queen. Now die." Marta raised both hands, and her eyes blazed blue. The princess stood to the side and screamed.

"No!"

Incredibly, Eleanor's eyes blazed a ferocious brown, and she lifted both hands at Marta, unleashing a torrent of brown fire. It struck and pinned the Dark Inner Circle Elf against the side of the throne. Marta screamed in anguish, trying to bring her blue fire to bear. As she struggled, Xander stood up.

"I also saved some, after all." He threw one last blue fireball at Marta. Combined with Princess Eleanor's brown stream of Power, it blew a gaping hole through the elf woman's chest. Marta's face froze in shock as she died. Xander fell to the ground, completely spent. Eleanor stopped her magic stream and looked in disbelief at her hands.

Morgo's stunned face turned to a sneer. He looked at the princess.

"I did not sense your magic. It must be the first time you broke your Wall and tasted the Power. You are the strongest Brown I have ever seen. It is a shame I cannot take you back with the others. You cannot take the life of an Inner Circle and live."

He reached out, and a dark energy surrounded the princess. Her eyes blazed brown in retaliation as she tried to push the blackness back. Morgo's eyes widened then hardened. Lifting his other hand, he increased his Power until she lifted off the ground. The black energy slowly compressed her brown magic back. The veins on his forehead stood out as he strained.

"Now, die!" he hissed, tightening his energy until it completely surrounded her. Eleanor cried out in pain, her petite body convulsing.

"No!" Chip screamed. He reached for more Power but found nothing. Morgo noticed how much she meant to him and laughed.

The boy flew deeper into his mind and found his spirit essence. It was a rolling ball of white energy suspended in the darkness. It was everything he was, nothing less, nothing more. He hesitated, knowing he would never be able to exist again.

"Don't do it!" Xander called faintly. He heard Morgo laugh louder as Eleanor screamed in agony.

It was then that the orphan chose to give everything.

The boy entered the white ball of light and filled himself with his spirit essence. From a distance, he heard the wizard scream in warning. Chip did not care anymore. He had given everything he had to get to this point, and now he was willing to sacrifice himself for the one he loved. The realization that he loved her made the boy smile. As love and white light filled him, something strange happened.

9

Time stopped. Chip saw Morgo's face frozen in a maniacal laugh, and then everything went white.

The entire world disappeared.

He turned around in disbelief and saw an old man sitting on a bench in a green park. For some reason, it did not bother him. He felt full of love and light. The boy felt at home.

"It is called an eternal moment," the man said in a rich voice. He had long silver hair and wore a white robe. Chip walked over and sat beside him. It felt like the right thing to do. He noticed beautiful trees in the park with smooth trunks and gorgeous green leaves. The grass was thick and luxurious. Silver birds flew overhead in the clear blue sky. A warm wind bathed his face, and he felt a peace he had never known.

"What moment?" he managed to ask. The old man looked at him with eyes of infinite depth.

"This moment. It can last forever. Tarry too long, though, and you might not wish to leave."

Chip nodded. It was not a threat, or a trick. It was just the way it was.

"Who are you?" he asked. "The Creator? Am I dead? Is this the end?"

The man with the silver hair let out a musical peal of laughter. Chip grinned despite everything.

"Such an inquisitive boy. You always were." He looked at him kindly, and his eyes crinkled with merriment. "The answer is no to all three." Chip looked confused. "Well, at least how humans see it."

"You mean how we view the Creator?" Chip asked in puzzlement. The old man raised his eyebrows.

"Do you remember when you encountered Death as a little boy? You were very ill and gave up on life." Chip looked down in shame. "Shame means we could not accept our vulnerability," he soothed. "True courage is not being afraid to be vulnerable."

Chip contemplated the statement. "I did not want to live anymore. I thought I had nothing and no one."

"What did the wizard show you?" the old man asked quietly.

"He showed me his life memories and how there were so many people, places, and things I had not experienced. I realized I wanted to live," the boy answered.

"Are you prepared to sacrifice all that for the princess?"

Chip paused. He looked sadly at the old man. "Yes."

The man with the silver hair nodded. "You are quite a remarkable young man."

Chip felt much better after the compliment. It was hard to stay sad in this place. "You never told me who you were?"

"Oh yes. Do you remember staying Death when he almost took you?" The boy nodded. "Well, he is a force that embodies the absence of life. I am his opposite." He leaned towards the orphan. Chip stared at him in wonder. The man's eyes up close were like pools of infinity. "I can tell you this. Death and Life cannot exist in the same spot." He stood up.

Chip grappled with the statement. He felt a sense of urgency as the old man rose. "If I use my spirit essence, what will happen to me?" he asked as the old man backed away. The park was starting to disappear.

"You will relinquish your Power and cease to exist in all ways," he said with finality. He started to fade away.

"But Morgo is made of Death. He can't die..." Chip struggled. The old man was almost gone.

"The bench does not move if you do not wish it to." The man with the silver hair disappeared. Everything went white except for the park bench. Chip stood in frustration, looking at it. His mind raced.

A thought was tugging at him, just out of reach. "What if ..." he mumbled, concentrating hard. "Of course!" He looked around one more time. The sense of peace was calling to him, and he began to doubt leaving at all. He knew if he wanted to, he could stay forever.

"No," he said, holding up his hand. "I have to save her." As he did with eternal Death, he did with eternal Life. The boy, filled with his spirit essence, pointed at the bench and tied a streak of white Power around its leg. Turning around, he re-entered his body as time unfroze.

The world materialized before him.

Blazing white light burst forth from his eyes. Gasps filled the throne room.

The demons in front fell and covered their faces, whining in terror. Morgo recoiled and released the princess from his death grip. His reptilian face hardened into a rictus of black hate. The general screamed at the boy and brought the full force of his Dark Energy to bear. Chip calmly lifted both hands and released his spirit essence at the black creature. A bright light exploded in the throne room as white energy surrounded General Morgo from head to foot.

The black mass inside him let out a desperate, otherworldly scream, carrying with it a lifetime of fear, greed, and lust for Power. The orphan, full of the greatest Power he had ever known, squeezed both hands. General Morgo wailed as the white energy compressed him. A host of otherworldly voices drowned out his cries as the portal to Death itself opened to pull him in forever. The black energy that was Morgo simply imploded and winked out of existence. His midnight black cloak fell to the ground empty. Life had reclaimed his being, and Death could not be in the same place. The Dark Energy was back where it belonged.

Chip instinctively followed the white rope of his spirit essence back to the leg of the bench beyond his Wall. He pulled the white light back into himself, knowing he had lost none. The boy had occupied the same spot as Death and it had no choice but to leave.

Chip knew using his spirit essence in that manner could only work on a creature like Morgo. It would be gone forever if he had expended it to fight someone else. The thought of losing his soul gave him a moment of infinite sadness. The boy looked at the bench. He momentarily thought the man with the silver hair was sitting on it, but the image faded. Chip withdrew from the ball of white energy in his mind. The light left his eyes, and his Wall snapped back into place. He stood light-headed and looked around him. Everyone was staring in stunned silence at what they had just witnessed. Even the demons still cowered uncertainly, faces fearful.

Suddenly, the door to the back of the throne room opened, and Miss Owl walked in. Her glasses slipped to the edge of her nose.

"Sorry I am late," she said, adjusting her glasses. "I must have overslept..." The room full of demons, soldiers, and magic wielders looked at her in surprise. "Oh dear."

The creatures in front stood up, realizing the hateful white light was gone. They mewled and snarled, then started moving forward.

"To me!" shouted the commander. "Get back behind the table!"

The demons poured out of the hallway into the throne room. No master was controlling them anymore, so their only impulse was to kill and feed. They looked at the humans hungrily. The ones in front reached over the table with their claws. A dozen soldiers were all that remained.

The weapons master began his dance of death. "Get to the escape tunnel," he called without turning. "We will follow when we can." Queen Charlotte and Princess Eleanor held each other while staggering towards the trap door. They both looked exhausted but determined. Chase tried to pick up Xander, who waved him off.

"I can manage myself, my boy. Go help Garth," he said without malice.

Chip stood in a daze. Miss Owl ran up and took his arm. He accepted her help. The queen tried to usher the princess down the hole, but Eleanor broke her grip and stumbled over to Chip.

"Thank you," she said, wrapping her arms tightly around him. Now, take us out of here." Despite his total exhaustion, he nodded and moved towards the escape route with a new purpose. The sound of fighting grew louder as more demons entered the throne room. They would soon be overrun.

The weapons master dealt out death with each stroke of his sword. His face was a piece of chiselled granite. Demons fell around him in piles, which slowed them down long enough for the others to go down the hatch. A larger demon smashed the overturned table and heaved it against the wall. The creatures formed a ring around the remaining men, and the circle tightened.

The survivors hacked their way to the steps of the throne, holding the demons back by sheer force of will. There seemed to be no end to them. Blood and saliva dripped off their fangs and claws. Chase ran down to help, and together, they pushed the creatures back long enough for everyone but the remaining soldiers to go down the tunnel.

Chip was about to enter after the princess but chose to stay and lend help. "All clear," he called, pulling his sword. Chase acknowledged him as a claw raked through and cut deep into his thigh. Another struck his shoulder.

Demons were feinting and slashing from all directions. Only six soldiers remained from the entire army, and most carried gashes and bite marks on different parts of their bodies. They were exhausted. One demon launched itself at a soldier on the outer edge of the shrinking circle and carried him into the milling mass on the other side. They tore him apart in seconds, increasing the frenzy. Only eight men in total were left, including the weapons master, Chase, and Chip.

"Go down," Garth ordered, blocking the thrusting demons.

"You first," panted Chase, decapitating a large demon before him.

"It's an order. Drop down the hole, men. Give me the room I need." The five soldiers leapt down one by one, not bothering to use the ladder. There was no time anyway. As they landed, the soldiers rolled to allow the next to fall. Finally, only Chip, Chase and the weapons master remained.

Demons attacked from all sides. They fought valiantly. The boys tried to drop through, but as soon as they killed a demon, another took its place. A sea of black, writhing bodies surrounded them. Shrieks filled the air. Garth was a blur of motion. The master and both apprentices danced the patterns of death, knowing exactly where the other would be. Years of training together had created a symbiosis of skill and technique. Every swipe or thrust of the sword left an opening or a weakness that the others filled until the dead demons piled around them. That finally gave the trio a moment to pause.

"Now," yelled Garth, and the boys leapt into the hole at the same time. The weapons master grabbed the trap door and pulled it shut as he dropped. Claws reached for him, but it closed in time. When he landed, they had already rolled out of the way.

"You said all at the same time," Chase grumbled.

Garth shrugged. "Someone had to close the trap door." He grinned and slapped the pair on the back. "You both did some good work up there. Now, let's get everybody out of here. The demons will soon figure out how to open that door."

Squire Longfellow led them to the others, waiting farther down the tunnel. The companions congratulated each other and started running down the damp stone corridor as best they could. The smell of earth and wet stone filled Chip's nose. The party had only one torch, which they had found in a sconce on the wall by the trap door. Eleanor grabbed his hand and ran beside him. They stayed together, afraid to be away from each other.

The group did not get very far before they heard a sound they were all dreading. The trap door slammed onto the floor of the throne room. As it hit the ground, the clang of metal reverberated down the long tunnel, sending chills through their veins. None of them, including the queen, knew exactly how far the passage extended.

The sounds of distant mewls and whines reached their ears. The magic wielders did not have enough strength to kill such a robust force. Despite Chase and the weapons master's abilities, they did not have enough men to defend them by hand. Everyone was injured or exhausted except Garth Stone. Chip could only marvel at his skill and endurance.

The sounds of pursuit grew louder, and the demons began to shriek and holler. It was pitch black in the tunnel behind them and beyond the torchlight in front. They were in a small circle of light running through an endless sea of darkness. The companions pushed each other, knowing they were only as fast as their slowest member. Their breathing grew ragged. Surely, the tunnel would end soon. Yet it did not.

The demons were almost upon them. Garth's face turned back to granite, and he yelled to the men, "To me. If we block the tunnel with bodies, we have a chance." He turned, and the soldiers stopped with him. "Run!" he commanded the others. "Find the end." Miss Owl threw the torch on the ground to give them light then lit her finger with a bit of yellow magic and led the way for the others.

It took only moments for the demons to catch up. One soldier went down on impact as the front demon skewered him with a frenzied attack using its four arms. Garth and Chase leapt forward and killed all the demons in the front. The ones behind tripped and fell over the dead bodies, causing a pile. The creatures behind struggled to get through the mass of writhing limbs. Gone was the discipline instilled in the creatures by the presence of their masters. In its place was a ravenous hunger fueled by madness and a need to kill. Their purpose was to tear into flesh, killing everything in their path to satisfy the insatiable need to feed. The men continued hacking at any appendage within reach. The demons behind were so frantic to get through that the pile of bodies pushed forward. The men had no choice but to back up. One of the four remaining soldiers in the back picked up the torch and held it aloft for the others.

"We found it!" Miss Owl screeched from a good distance down the tunnel. The mass of dead bodies continued to push against them. They retreated and saw the light of Miss Owl's finger at the end of the tunnel.

"We cannot open it," she called. "It must be stuck."

The pile of bodies continued pushing forward.

"We have to do something," Chip said, his anxiety rising. He did not like tight places. The weight of the rock around the tunnel seemed to press down on him. The moving mass of live and dead demons was now visible in Miss Owl's small circle of light, creeping inexorably closer. The live ones stuck in the middle were ready to rake anything with their claws. Miss Owl climbed the ladder at the end of the tunnel and tried to send lances of yellow magic into the trap door, but it did nothing.

Xander stepped forward. "Morgo must have done something to it when he entered, just in case. It will take much magic to open." He strained to produce blue fire, but it sputtered out.

"Wait," called the princess. She stepped forward. "I am a Brown, and I think I am strong enough for this. I feel a connection to the earth." Xander moved aside.

"Um, you might want to hurry," Chase said, pointing to the moving mass of bodies almost upon them.

Princess Eleanor concentrated, and her eyes blazed bright brown. Chip could feel the peculiar crackling of magic. She raised her hands, and ribbons of brown Power reached up and pushed against the trap door. It did not open. She strained then stopped.

They were now huddled close to one another. The reek of demon bodies filled their nostrils. A soldier at the back screamed as a clawed hand pulled him back into the melee. Sharp fangs bit into his neck from both sides, lapping up his blood.

Eleanor tried to remain calm. "I know what to do." She focused again and pointed at the earth around the trap door. Raising both hands in an upward gesture, the princess released a thick stream of brown energy into the ground around the door. The earth trembled then lifted up in a circle around the ladder, carrying the trap door with it. She tossed the huge mound sideways, and a blast of cool night air hit them. They all drew in deep breaths greedily.

"Move!" shouted Garth, but they needed no further motivation. Miss Owl went up the ladder as quickly as she ever moved, followed by the queen, Eleanor and the squire. Xander went next, and then Chip and Chase followed suit. The weapons master had no choice but to race up as the mass of demons pushed his soldiers into him. He climbed to the top and leaned down the hole to pull up the remaining men, one at a time. The last man paused to slice the arm off of a large demon about to disembowel him then tried to climb up. The pile of demons was now directly under him. Garth tried to clasp his hand to pull him up, but several demons grabbed his legs and yanked him backwards. He fell straight down into the milling mass below.

The poor soldier tried to climb again, but clawed hands wrapped around him and started tearing. Sharp fangs tore into him from all sides, and his whole body erupted in fountains of blood. Garth made a sign to the Creator, and the party stepped back, realizing the demons were trying to follow them out. The companions had emerged from the tunnel a few hundred feet from the eastern city wall in a small thicket of trees. It was a cool autumn night.

They could hear the screams of the demons below, fighting to climb up the ladder. The first one leapt out of the hole and landed on the soft forest floor. Garth decapitated the creature, and its headless body fell back down the shaft, briefly slowing the ascent of the others.

Eleanor stepped forward, her eyes still blazing brown. Several more demons spilled out. Garth and Chase sliced them to pieces, but more kept trying to emerge. The princess pointed both hands at the mound of earth beside the tunnel hole. Brown ropes of magic infused the ground, and she raised her arms, lifting the entire heap.

The princess shook from the strain, and the other magic wielders knew she was still exhausted from her battle with Morgo. She moved her hands sideways, and the whole mound of dirt floated over the gaping hole. Several demons were scampering up at once, desperately trying to reach the humans. The creatures shrieked at them with fangs bared. Eleanor dropped her arms, and the entire mound fell on the emerging demons, crushing them and filling the whole shaft with dirt. The tunnel became a tomb. The princess staggered back from the effort. Everyone sank down with relief. Chip held the petite girl while she recovered.

"Well, that settles that," Chase said, trying to sound cheerful. He was drenched in sweat and blood. The tall boy sat down, taking deep breaths. His father looked at his son with pride. They were down to a group of ten, all that remained of Vanalon.

The weapons master sheathed his sword. "The surviving demons will backtrack down the tunnel and enter the throne room. From there the smarter ones may be able to determine where we came out. Either way they will search around the city walls to find our trail. I am afraid this is not over. By my guess, there are still over fifty demons alive. We cannot defeat them on open ground if they come for us all at once. We need to leave the valley immediately." They all nodded soberly.

Garth looked at the two remaining soldiers. They were both young but well-trained. "You have fought bravely, Marcus and Gavin. I want you to tell your children and grandchildren this tale. We may have lost the city for now, but the enemy has paid dearly. The Demon King lost his general, two Inner Circle members, and his black dragon. Not to mention a thousand demons. That will give them pause and buy us time to put together a proper army. We gave everything today, but I refuse to give any more of our lives. We must go now."

They all got to their feet, feeling inspired. Chip helped Eleanor up, who had sat down to recover. The party trekked east and found the One Road leading out of the valley. It was early evening, and the sounds of nightlife surrounded them. They looked at each other, feeling a huge relief to feel the open air after the confines of the tunnel. The smell of trees and grass permeated everything, and for a moment, it was easy to forget that demons were crawling through the city, searching for survivors. They made good headway for a while, moving at a slow jog. Then yelps erupted far behind them, followed by shrieks and bellows.

"They have found the tunnel exit and our scent. Run!" whispered the weapons master. They all took off down the One Road as fast as they could. The group made sure not to outpace their slowest runner, Queen Charlotte. Miss Owl and Eleanor kept pace with her, offering encouragement, even though they were also exhausted. Long moments went by, and the sounds of pursuit intensified. Their breathing became more ragged. An entire day of fighting had depleted everyone. There was a hill in the road up ahead.

"Let's get to the top and make our stand there. We can at least fight from higher ground," Garth said grimly. He had a rare look of frustration as he realized this was the end. His features then turned to granite, and cold steel shone in his eyes as he prepared to deal death one last time.

When they reached the top of the hill, Garth Stone stopped and unsheathed his sword. He unbuckled his belt and threw it to the side. The weapons master then walked to the middle of the One Road and turned to face the oncoming demons. His eyes had a strange anticipatory glint as if he relished the challenge.

The High Commander of Vanalon gave them his final instructions. "Change of plans. All of you take the boy to safety. He is the prophecy and the one hope. Everything is lost if he falls. I will hold them off as long as I can." They tried to interrupt. "Go now!" he commanded in a voice like thunder.

Xander nodded sadly and placed a hand on his Protector's shoulder. Miss Owl used her small Power to light the bushes on fire at each side of the road so he could see. The shrieking mob of demons was now a large, dark blob running full speed towards them in the distance.

"Run!" Xander ordered. They all turned and ran over the top of the hill. Chip turned back in anguish to look at the man who had trained him most of his life.

Garth Stone stood silhouetted in the light of the burning bushes on the One Road east of the deserted city of Vanalon. He bristled with all manner of weapons. In his left hand was a dagger, and in the right a sword. Across his back was an axe. Strapped along his legs were sharp blades and other implements of death. He would use them as necessary. The commander stood with feet apart, bracing for his final fight. Over fifty demons emerged into the light cast by the burning bushes, hurtling towards him, eager to tear him apart. The front ones screamed with glee as they went in for what they thought was an easy kill. But they miscalculated, for he was the weapons master.

10

Chip tried to wipe away tears that came unbidden to his cheeks as he ran down the hill. The man was as much a father to him as a trainer. A small voice in his head said Garth would kill them all. He was the greatest. Yet the boy knew deep down that not even the weapons master could survive an assault of such a large force in the open. He wanted to turn back and help, but he knew it was taking everything he had to put one foot in front of the other, trying to make Garth's sacrifice worth it.

They ran down the first hill and up the next. So far, there were no sounds of pursuit. Chip was so tired that forcing his limbs to go further was difficult. The others were experiencing the same exhaustion. Despite it all, he became angry that he had given everything, and it might not be enough.

The man with the silver hair seemed to offer so much hope, but, in the end, the demons would likely catch them anyway. His steps faltered, but Chase caught him before he fell. Even his best friend breathed heavily and had no energy for his customary jokes. Chip lifted his head and saw another hill looming before him. He did not think he would make it. The others staggered upward, everyone fighting their personal battles. He looked up at the stars in the black night sky. They looked so peaceful. He wanted to give up.

"Never give up," he heard the weapons master say in his mind. "Above all else, never give up."

Tears streamed down Chip's face. He had struggled his whole life. The boy had promised himself he would never give up again, but now everything was gone—Vanalon, Garth Stone, even his Power. It would be so easy to finally fall down.

Never give up.

The thought repeated in his head, over and over.

He decided to honour the weapons master. He would give himself no choice. Besides, he had given his word. The boy looked up and pushed harder, finally cresting the hill. Somehow, he had passed the others. He looked ahead at the land below him and froze.

His companions came up behind and stopped.

A long string of lights came up the hill towards them. The sound of horses' hooves thudded in the distance. The ground began to vibrate. Be it friend or foe, they stood waiting. The horses galloped to the top of the hill, where they stood.

"Who goes there?" the man on the lead horse said. He was wearing an eagle insignia. Xander broke into a grin.

"Well met, Captain Peters," the wizard said in welcome. "You are a sight for sore eyes." He turned to the others. "The Calgars are here."

The captain laughed. "It's been a while, Xander. You look a sorry lot if I may be blunt." He then saw the queen and princess. "My apologies, Your Highnesses. I did not see you." His face took on a note of fear. "What has befallen Vanalon?"

The wizard stepped forward. "Vanalon has fallen, but it is not lost. Our brave High Commander Garth Stone defends us from a horde of demons as we speak. Please give me one hundred of your best cavalry and ten mounts. He may yet live." The captain nodded and issued orders, which passed down the line.

Ten cavalrymen leapt off their horses without question and helped them up. Chip struggled onto an empty mount. Chase and the others did the same. Three wizards rode up wearing yellow and brown robes.

The brown-robed magic wielder was an older woman with a youthful face. "Grand Wizard Xander, we come in your time of need."

The wizard turned his mount and smiled broadly. "Hello, Miriam. We do need your help. There is not much time." He nodded at the two younger wizards wearing yellow robes. "Please follow." He spurred his horse forward down the road, riding hard. The one hundred men followed, hooves thundering. Chip pushed aside all exhaustion as best he could, feeling a renewed wave of excitement course through him. Maybe there was still a chance.

They crested the second hill back towards Vanalon and saw the horde of demons surrounding something in the light of the burning bushes. In the middle, there seemed to be a flurry of movement. Hearing the horses, the demons turned, baring their fangs. Seeing new flesh, they raced full force at the cavalry. The men from Calgar were not used to the sight of the creatures and pulled up in fear.

"Swords out," Captain Peters yelled. "They bleed and die like all of us," he said with a proper commanding tone, but even he looked shocked. Fortunately, there were less than twenty demons left. The men surrounded them with the horses and hacked them to pieces. The wizards used their magic to finish off those that remained. Several animals went down, including three Calgar soldiers. Chip raced around the melee to find Garth.

Dead bodies littered the area, some piled three high. At least thirty demons were dead. In the middle of the One Road lay the weapons master. His head rested on the leg of one of the dead demons. Chip leapt off his horse and ran to his teacher's side. Garth was covered with wounds from head to foot. His face though looked peaceful. The commander's eyes were closed. He still clasped his sword in his right hand. All his weapons had been used before he went down, now sticking out of various demons. He had put up a fight for the ages. Tears of pride filled Chip's eyes.

"Takes more than that," Garth grunted, opening one eye. The boy gasped. "Don't get too excited... They still got me." Blood leaked out of the corner of his mouth. The others rushed up and began offering words of encouragement. Xander knelt beside him, turning pale, then called the other three wizards over.

"He is grievously wounded. Link together and try healing him." The two Yellows and one Brown put their hands over one another on Garth's bloody chest. Their eyes shone with bright magic as their combined Power entered the weapons master. Several long moments passed before Miriam looked up in resignation, shaking her head.

"Such pain. I am afraid he is too far gone. He's slipping away."

"No!" Chip cried out. He put his hand over hers. "Don't give up!" he shouted to all of them, including the weapons master. Garth's lips seemed to twitch.

Xander put his hand over Chip's, trying to hide his doubt. "We don't have much, but let's give everything we can." Queen Charlotte and Princess Eleanor added their hands. Miss Owl slid off her horse and scuttled over to them.

She put her hand over theirs. "Let me try," Miss Owl insisted. Miriam looked at her dubiously, but Xander nodded. "Focus, all of you. Let me direct your Power."

Chip broke through the Wall in his mind and thankfully found a small measure of red Power rebuilding itself. He channelled it to Miss Owl. Curiously, by linking, he could feel the strength of Power in each of them and how much they had in reserve. The Power of the princess amazed him. She was almost equal to Xander, even though she was only a Brown. For now, they had little in reserve.

At that moment, Garth Stone stopped breathing.

Miss Owl paused, took a deep breath, then expertly fused their Power and sank it into the weapons master. She recoiled at the extent of the damage then immediately started his heart, which beat irregularly. She went to work mending and reforming. Miss Owl stopped the bleeding on the outside first, closing all gashes and restoring the skin. She entered his veins and repaired them with precision. The schoolteacher then delved deep into his body, healing damaged organs and mending broken ribs. His lung had ruptured, but she pulled the soft tissue together, making it grow and fuse. Some of them used all their Power and began dropping out of the link one by one.

Finally, she reached the weapons master's damaged heart, which had a laceration. There was almost no Power left. Even Xander fell away until it was just her and Chip. Grunting from the effort, she took the final measure of Power from the boy and, adding her last bit of magic, mended the laceration until it disappeared. Miss Owl promptly fell over and passed out. Chip fell to the other side but managed to stay conscious. Everyone waited, not saying a word. Looks of dismay clouded their faces as the weapons master lay still, not moving.

Then his chest raised, and he took a full, deep breath. Both eyes opened.

"Where is my sword?"

They all laughed weakly and patted each other on the back. Miss Owl stirred, then sat up, pushing her glasses back up her nose.

"Oh good, it worked," she chirped happily. They all slumped down amid the wreckage of bodies. Captain Peters dropped beside them. By now, the entire army was there to assist. Soldiers brought chairs and cleared the bodies. Garth was able to stand long enough to take a chair. He would need several days to recover, Miss Owl scolded, and nothing less. All of them would need time to recuperate. The Calgars brought out hunks of cheese and bread for them to eat, which they accepted gratefully. Chip had never felt so hungry.

"What is the next step?" asked the captain.

Xander took a mug of ale offered by one of the soldiers before answering. "The city is empty. You may find a few stray demons here and there, but the main army has been defeated. My advice is to refortify Vanalon. Fix the gates first. Make it look like we intend to defend it again. The Demon King is cunning. He will know that with a handful of men, we took out General Morgo, two Inner Circle, and his black dragon. I hope he will assume the same people will stay to fight, awaiting reinforcements, including myself. He will not attack again unless victory is assured. That means several Inner Circle members plus a much larger army. He may even come himself or wait until the barrier falls.

"We achieved our goal and bought something very precious, more time. Occupying the city will make him pause and regroup. Have sentries posted to report any large movements. When he amasses enough demons and magic wielders, he will attack. That may take a few weeks or longer if we are lucky. You must be ready at all times. When he marches, you can determine if you want to mount a brief defence or abandon the city, heading for Calgar, where you can make a proper stand. By then, we will have fortified it with troops from Toron and extra magic wielders."

Captain Peters nodded. "It makes sense. Who will command Vanalon?"

Xander responded. "King Rupert perished in the attack." Charlotte and Eleanor looked down. They had not had time to grieve. The captain offered his condolences. "In the interim," the wizard continued, "Queen Charlotte will resume command until Eleanor is of age." He looked at the queen, who nodded.

"I will fulfill my oath to reign until the city falls or is relinquished to save lives and ensure a better defence from Calgar. I will also organize what should be removed for safekeeping." Charlotte looked wistful, realizing how much she had lost.

Xander agreed. "Abandoning the city at the right time may save it for the future. The demons are single-minded. They are not interested in destroying or burning unless ordered as part of an attack. They also hate fire. A demon's dual purpose is to kill and eat. They will likely pass through an empty city. Vanalon may yet survive. However, this plan is not without risk. There is a chance the demon army will catch up to you before reaching Calgar. If so, you must have an established strategy to defend yourselves."

"It sounds like you will not be with us," Captain Peters inferred.

"No." The wizard shook his head. "It is too dangerous for me and some others to stay here. We have essential tasks to fulfill to prepare for the invasion." Eleanor looked up with concern on her face.

"Am I coming with you?" the princess asked, glancing from Chip to Xander.

The wizard sighed. "That is up to your mother. Coming with us would endanger you. The demons and Dark Elves will search for us relentlessly, especially if they do not see me in the city. Anyone accompanying us will be in grave danger. I do admit staying in Vanalon has its risks, princess. There is always a chance that the demons will make a surprise attack or chase you down if the city is not abandoned in time. Also, everyone needs to be vigilant for assassin demons. They are furtive and can slip in undetected. The guards must be especially aware of that risk. Another option is for you to travel with us to Calgar and remain there until your mother joins you. Fortune willing, we will all meet up in Toron in less than ninety days for the convening of the High Council."

The queen considered. It was apparent that Princess Eleanor wanted to stay with Chip, but she remained silent. After a few moments, Charlotte's face showed she had reached a decision. Chip's heart sped up, but he did not move.

"I feel it is important for my daughter and me to meet in Toron to represent Vanalon at the High Council. Despite the risks, I would prefer she accompanies you to the capital and act as regent if I cannot arrive in time." Eleanor let out a sigh of relief. "Besides, I cannot think of better people to protect her." She smiled and put her hand on her daughter's shoulder. "She is all I have left. Please keep her safe."

The wizard bowed his head. "As you command, Queen of Vanalon. I agree with your analysis. The princess has demonstrated certain abilities that I would like to study. All right, it is settled."

Someone cleared her throat delicately. Miss Owl pushed her glasses up and peered at the queen with large, bright eyes.

Charlotte looked over and smiled. "It would be a delight if you could keep me company too, Miss Owl. If you wish, of course." The teacher beamed. Despite the harrowing escape, Miss Owl still kept her sweater neatly buttoned and shawl clasped. "And you, Squire Longfellow. It would be near impossible to catalogue things without your help."

Chase's father smiled at the queen and bowed low. "It would be an honour."

"As you wish," Xander acknowledged, trying to hide his amusement. He looked around, eyes settling on the two soldiers who had survived. "Marcus and Gavin, you have displayed the highest level of courage and bravery. With the queen's blessing, I would ask that you both receive a promotion."

Charlotte turned to the two men. "I thank you for your service and offer you positions in the Queen's Guard until you assume dual command of the future Vanalon army, the Creator willing."

Marcus turned to Gavin, and they shared a look. "We will always hold to our oath. It would be an honour to serve in the Queen's Guard and assume command as you see fit," Gavin said. Before this, they were merely foot soldiers. A promotion of this magnitude came rarely. The queen smiled and stood to put a hand on both of their shoulders.

"Good choice." The wizard smiled at them and then looked at his Protector, who was still sitting quietly but listening. "Will you be ready to travel in the morning?"

The weapons master looked at the wizard sourly. "A few cuts and scrapes are not going to slow me down. We can leave now if you wish." The others smiled. Chase stifled a laugh.

"That will not be necessary, my good Protector. I think we all deserve a full night's rest." He looked at Captain Peters. "If it pleases you, may we spend the night in extra tents? We wish to travel to Calgar in the morning."

The captain bowed his head. "You may have the command tent for this evening. It is much larger and more comfortable. I can have a detachment remain behind to keep guard. We can carry on to the city if it pleases the queen."

"In other circumstances, I would say yes, good captain. However, I am already falling asleep on my feet. I also recommend entering the city during the day. We do not know if stray demons are lurking about in the night. The city should be scoured before we occupy it."

The captain agreed. "As you command, Queen Charlotte. We will all camp here tonight and depart on our separate journeys in the morning." He got to his feet and started issuing orders.

Men ran to unload the equipment from wagons, and a short time later, tents sprang up in a wide area. The command tent took longer but was worth the wait. It was a large structure with several rooms. A soldier lit a small brazier in the main seating area, providing heat to ward off the chill. A small hole in the top provided an escape from the smoke. Carpets covered the main living areas, and cots were set up with goose-down blankets in the various rooms.

The weary party chose their beds and began undressing. The soldiers delivered hot wash basins for the guests. The women chose one of the back rooms with three cots and closed their partition. Chip heard Queen Charlotte saying she intuitively knew her daughter would be a magic wielder one day. The boy tried to undress and wash but only managed to remove his coat and boots before pushing the blankets over to lie down for a moment. He immediately fell into a deep sleep.

Chip awoke to soft voices coming from the main living area. A bright light illuminated the thick walls of the tent. He gingerly sat up. Everything hurt, but it was now a dull pain, and his main exhaustion was gone. He got up and relieved himself in a small room designed for that task. When the boy walked into the command tent's main living area, the rest of the party greeted him heartily. His face showed only slight guilt for being the last to awake.

"Sorry for sleeping late. Did you all have breakfast?" he asked sheepishly.

They smiled. "We are about to have lunch," Chase laughed. Chip's eyes widened.

"I slept until lunch? I'm so sorry."

Xander chuckled. "No need, my boy. The Creator decides how much you sleep, not us. I am glad you rested well. Let's eat, and then we must be off."

The Calgar soldiers brought in steaming, heaping plates of food. Chip received venison stew over boiled potatoes and slices of fresh side bread with cheese. Ale and cold stream water were on offer to accompany the delicious meal. He decided to have a glass of each. The orphan did not wait for the food to cool before eating ravenously.

Xander looked over. "Use of magic makes you hungry," he commented with a smile, "Eat up." Chip did not have to be told twice. He accepted a second plate and wolfed it down. Chase, not to be outdone, managed to eat three plates.

When finished, new basins of hot water arrived. They washed and put on the new garments provided. Their old clothes had been cleaned while they bathed and somehow mysteriously dried. The wizard came out with a mended blue robe and a twinkle in his eye. Chip looked at him.

"I thought we were supposed to use it only when absolutely necessary?" the boy said accusatorily, trying to hide a grin.

"My goodness, it was necessary. Do you see any blue robes lying about?" he laughed. His hair and beard were neatly trimmed, and the dark circles had left his eyes. "If you are ready, let us be off. We have a long journey."

The others gathered outside as the soldiers dismantled the command tent.

Queen Charlotte hugged her daughter in a long embrace. "The Creator willing, we will see each other at the High Council," she said, eyes brimming.

"I will be fine," Princess Eleanor said, holding her tight.

Chase's father gave his son a huge bear hug. "You did well, my boy. Come back in one piece."

Chase looked shocked that he would come back in any other way. "I certainly hope so." Everyone laughed.

When they had all said their goodbyes, Captain Peters stepped forward. Queen Charlotte, Miss Owl, and the two remaining Vanalon soldiers, Marcus and Gavin, stood behind him. The Calgar soldiers were all packed, mounted and standing in a long column stretching down the road. "We wish you all a safe journey, Xander and company." Chip, Chase, Eleanor, and the weapons master stood beside the wizard. "Do you wish a detachment of soldiers to accompany you?"

Xander shook his head. "I fear it would draw unwanted attention. Besides, I believe we are sufficiently rested to handle ourselves. Thank you for the supplies. They are much appreciated. I wish you and your men the best of luck. You have a dangerous task ahead of you. It will be critical to time it right. I ask that you provide your three magic wielders with blue robes. The enemy scouts should assume it is me, plus others from the Guild. This will give the Demon King pause. He will withhold his army until it is strong enough, buying us more time. You will find many dead in the city. Please provide the men who died defending Vanalon a proper burial."

"Of course, Grand Wizard. The men will be honoured. Travel well." He saluted.

They all waved, and the Calgars started marching as one down the road towards Vanalon, led by the captain riding beside the queen. The companions watched as the contingent passed by and grew smaller in the distance.

Above them, far to the west, dark clouds were massing. A storm was coming. When the army was out of sight, the small party of five turned and looked down the empty One Road to the east. The sun shone bright, and the air was fresh. They felt their hearts lift with hope.

"To the Wizard's Guild," Xander said, trying not to smile.

They all looked at him. "Are we not going to Calgar?" asked Chase with a furrowed brow.

The wizard looked at him shrewdly. "That is where they think we are going. If Dark Elves capture any soldiers or villagers, they will point the demons towards Calgar. I intend to take a different path. They can still track us, but it should throw them off for a while. Besides, we have important business in the Guild. My brother, the High Wizard, would like to meet you, Chip."

He kicked the flanks of his horse.

The others spread out on the One Road and kept pace. Chip

looked ahead in wonder. He had never travelled east from Vanalon before. The boy looked sideways at the princess, who smiled at him. They were about to embark on the adventure he always dreamed about. The orphan took a deep breath and looked straight ahead at the empty road. He felt ready.

End of Volume 2.

IF YOU ENJOYED READING THIS, please leave a review on Amazon. It would be greatly appreciated.

Visit my website: www.terryironwood.com

Type your email address at the bottom of the page to be notified of my next book launch.

I have added a free short story prequel called "Weapons Master" in the upper right corner of my website. It is Garth Stone's backstory.

The Orphan's Quest audiobook with special effects is now available on Audible.

Link to Volume Three: A Dim World

I hope you enjoyed Volume 2: Defenders of Hope. Be sure to look out for Volumes 3 to 7 of The Great Forget Fantasy Series!

The Great Forget Fantasy Series:

Volume 1: Orphan's Quest

Volume 2: Defenders of Hope

Volume 3: A Dim World

Volume 4: Guardian

Volume 5: Wizard's Guild

Volume 6: Stone Kingdom

Volume 7: Coming end of December, 2024.

Acknowledgements

I offer my heartfelt thanks to my family and friends, who provided invaluable support, wisdom, and encouragement. You know who you are. I especially want to mention Kevin C., Steve S., and Ward C., who went above and beyond.

I am delighted to work with my editor, Jason Letts from Imbue Editing, who continues to improve my writing.

Last, and certainly not least, I wish to thank an orphan, Chip, for taking me on his quest.

Many thanks,

Terry Ironwood

ABOUT THE AUTHOR

Terry Ironwood resides with his family. He holds multiple university degrees and is interested in the science of self-improvement. He is equally fascinated with physics and spirituality. Terry believes in an 'attitude of gratitude' and is grateful he can write full-time. His dream is to help others reach their full potential.

Printed in Dunstable, United Kingdom